P9-DOH-320

Once outside the RV, the woman tried to run

When Bolan caught hold of her again, she fought, launching martial-arts kicks and swinging her manacled fists. Slipping behind her, the Executioner looped his free arm under her chin and put her in a sleeper hold. Seconds later she passed out and he caught her limp form.

After securing the woman in the passenger seat and duct-taping her hands behind her, Bolan slid behind the steering wheel. He surveyed the battle zone, knowing the Border Patrol and the Arizona State Police would arrive soon.

As he got under way, the soldier glanced at the unconscious woman beside him, wondering what secrets she held and how they might tie in with three Russian nuclear weapons that had gone missing somewhere off the coast of China.

MACK BOLAN ®
The Executioner

DON PENDLETON'S
EXECUTIONER®
THE
NUCLEAR GAME

The
Moon Shadow
Trilogy
Book I

A GOLD EAGLE BOOK FROM
WORLDWIDE®

TORONTO • NEW YORK • LONDON
AMSTERDAM • PARIS • SYDNEY • HAMBURG
STOCKHOLM • ATHENS • TOKYO • MILAN
MADRID • WARSAW • BUDAPEST • AUCKLAND

If you purchased this book without a cover you should be aware
that this book is stolen property. It was reported as "unsold and
destroyed" to the publisher, and neither the author nor the
publisher has received any payment for this "stripped book."

First edition July 2003
ISBN 0-373-64296-2

Special thanks and acknowledgment to
Mel Odom for his contribution to this work.

NUCLEAR GAME

Copyright © 2003 by Worldwide Library.

All rights reserved. Except for use in any review, the
reproduction or utilization of this work in whole or in part
in any form by any electronic, mechanical or other means,
now known or hereafter invented, including xerography,
photocopying and recording, or in any information storage
or retrieval system, is forbidden without the written permission
of the publisher, Worldwide Library, 225 Duncan Mill Road,
Don Mills, Ontario, Canada M3B 3K9.

All characters in this book have no existence outside the
imagination of the author and have no relation whatsoever to
anyone bearing the same name or names. They are not even
distantly inspired by any individual known or unknown to the
author, and all incidents are pure invention.

® and TM are trademarks of the publisher. Trademarks indicated
with ® are registered in the United States Patent and Trademark
Office, the Canadian Trade Marks Office and in other countries.

Printed in U.S.A.

I dreamt the past was never past redeeming:
But whether this was false or honest dreaming
I beg death's pardon now...

—Richard Purdy Wilbur
The Pardon (1950)

It's never too late to repent. Redemption is possible
if it comes from the heart. But it takes strength and
true conviction.

—Mack Bolan

THE
MACK BOLAN®
LEGEND

Nothing less than a war could have fashioned the destiny of the man called Mack Bolan. Bolan earned the Executioner title in the jungle hell of Vietnam.

But this soldier also wore another name—Sergeant Mercy. He was so tagged because of the compassion he showed to wounded comrades-in-arms and Vietnamese civilians.

Mack Bolan's second tour of duty ended prematurely when he was given emergency leave to return home and bury his family, victims of the Mob. Then he declared a one-man war against the Mafia.

He confronted the Families head-on from coast to coast, and soon a hope of victory began to appear. But Bolan had broken society's every rule. That same society started gunning for this elusive warrior—to no avail.

So Bolan was offered amnesty to work within the system against terrorism. This time, as an employee of Uncle Sam, Bolan became Colonel John Phoenix. With a command center at Stony Man Farm in Virginia, he and his new allies—Able Team and Phoenix Force—waged relentless war on a new adversary: the KGB.

But when his one true love, April Rose, died at the hands of the Soviet terror machine, Bolan severed all ties with Establishment authority.

Now, after a lengthy lone-wolf struggle and much soul-searching, the Executioner has agreed to enter an "arm's-length" alliance with his government once more, reserving the right to pursue personal missions in his Everlasting War.

Prologue

South China Sea, 1797

"You know they will kill us all if they catch us."

Chi-Kan Zhao glanced at the ship cutting through the ocean less than a quarter mile from his fishing boat. In the distance, the junk's white sails stood out against the dark night sky and the sea. The emperor's flag, a yellow triangle with a green dragon, fluttered from the main mast.

"If the Chia-ch'ing emperor's men catch us," Chi-Kan agreed, "then they will kill us and put our heads on pikes for all to see. Therefore, we must make certain that they do not catch us."

Pak-Hong shook his head. He was older than Chi-Kan, already past his middle years and breaking down from long, hard years spent fighting the capricious sea, unrelenting sun and harsh weather. Like Chi-Kan, Pak-Hong wore black clothing so he wouldn't be easily seen at night.

"Your new friend will bring death and doom to us all," Pak-Hong whispered.

Chi-Kan knew his old friend spoke softly so that his new friend couldn't overhear him. Glancing toward the stern of the fishing boat, Chi-Kan saw Soo-Duk standing near the man handling the tiller.

Soo-Duk was younger, almost young enough to be Chi-Kan's son, only three years older than Sung-Hee, who was Chi-Kan's oldest boy. Standing thin and tall, Soo-Duk reminded Chi-Kan of a sword always held in readiness. Everything about the man was neat and orderly. Soo-Duk had an easy smile, but Chi-Kan had noted that the smile never touched the man's eyes.

Once, Chi-Kan remembered, he had been as fastidious about his appearance as the younger man. Then he had gotten married and become a father four times over. In the beginning of his marriage, fishing had been good. He and his wife hadn't made much money, but they hadn't needed much money. Now, with all the mouths at home to feed and the way the emperor kowtowed to the wealthy and the privileged throughout the empire, a poor man could no longer remain an honest man without starving.

Steadily, with the wind at their backs, coming up on the cargo junk at an oblique angle, the fishing boat caught up with its prey.

Despite his reservations about his present endeavor, Chi-Kan found his heart beating more rapidly in anticipation that made him feel guilty. If Soo-Duk were correct in what the merchant ships out of Hainan carried, the cargo aboard the junk could be enough to help Chi-Kan feed his family through the lean months ahead. Fishing, in most of the heavily fished ports where there was deep and safe water, had grown scant from too many fishermen and too many hungry mouths. He prayed that the gods would favor him.

"Chi-Kan," Pak-Hong pleaded, "we are not pirates. Not yet. It is not too late to turn around and be done with this." Tears glinted in his eyes.

Shaking his head and hardening his heart, Chi-Kan said, "No. We have cast our lot. If you had felt so strongly about this when we first set sail, you should have stayed with the others." The other ship's crew consisted of two of Chi-Kan's sons and one young man who would never have thought of becoming a pirate.

Only old Pak-Hong and five fishermen Chi-Kan had known for years had agreed to the night run. Soo-Duk had brought two men he knew—two men well versed in pirating, he promised—to round out the ten-man crew. Ten men, Soo-Duk had said, could move quickly enough to take a merchant ship.

Soo-Duk came forward. He carried two swords through the sash around his waist, as well as a brace of flintlock pistols on a leather shoulder strap. During the evening of conversation over rice wine three days ago, Soo-Duk had let Chi-Kan hold one of the pistols. A short time later, while they were both feeling the effects of the wine, Soo-Duk had let Chi-Kan shoot the pistol at targets floating out in the water.

Before that night, Chi-Kan had never touched a pistol. After that night, he could never imagine not wanting such a weapon. Holding the pistol, sighting down the barrel and shooting something made him feel powerful, more of a man than he had felt about being a father and a fisherman in years.

"Are you ready?" Soo-Duk asked as the fishing boat swiftly overtook the junk.

"Yes," Chi-Kan answered.

Soo-Duk took one of his pistols from the strap and handed the weapon to Chi-Kan. "I want you to carry this into battle tonight. For luck. A gift from me to you."

"I could not accept such a thing," Chi-Kan said. But he reached for the pistol anyway. What he said was only words and they both knew that. He loved the heaviness of the pistol, the smooth feel of the stock.

"I ask that you accept the gift," Soo-Duk said. "Aboard that ship, the sailors may develop streaks of bravery. If you shoot a man, shoot to kill him. You may save the lives of other men that don't have to die."

Chi-Kan nodded. They had discussed this before. "I will not fail you, Soo-Duk."

The younger man grinned in the weak moonlight. "Nor will I fail you, my new friend. Let's take this ship and see if the cargo is as fine as I believe it to be."

Chi-Kan was surprised at how quickly everything seemed to happen. In only minutes, the fishing boat drew abreast of the junk. Soo-Duk and his two companions whirled padded grappling hooks over their heads and cast them toward the junk less than fifteen feet away. Laden by cargo, the junk only floated a couple of feet higher than the fishing boat.

"Now," Soo-Duk ordered, leaping onto one of the grappling ropes and starting across.

Chi-Kan grabbed one of the ropes, as well, praying that the end lashed to his fishing boat didn't harm the vessel. His heart hammered in his chest, threatening to explode like the fireworks set off in the city on the emperor's birthday.

Seconds later, Chi-Kan dropped to the surging deck of the junk. Where were the sailors? Didn't the men know they were in waters infested by pirates? The deck was barely lit by two whale-oil lanterns that scattered the shadows only a little and burned orange against the night.

Pak-Hong dropped to the deck, as well. Chi-Kan was surprised the old man had possessed the strength to make the climb across the open water.

"Boarders!" someone yelled. "Pirates!"

Turning, Chi-Kan spotted a shadow rousing from the prow. Evidently the man supposed to be on watch had fallen asleep.

The hue and cry filled the junk. Men clambered up from belowdecks, brandishing cutlasses and knives. Two carried lanterns that made them targets for Soo-Duk's pistols.

Chi-Kan stood ready, the pistol in one hand and the cutlass in the other. He smelled the salt of the sea in the air and felt the thrum of blood against his temples.

"Put down your weapons!" Soo-Duk roared. "Put down your weapons and you won't be harmed!"

Foul curses followed his words, spoken by the sailors of the junk who didn't believe him. Pirates in the Hainan area weren't known for treating prisoners well. Some said dying was far better than depending on pirates for mercy.

"Die, damn you!" someone yelled.

A pistol burst flame from the stern of the ship. Chi-Kan threw himself to the deck, knowing the shot had come from a man in the raised tiller section. Soo-Duk turned, lifted another of his pistols and fired instantly. The bullet caught the man in the upper body and flipped him over the ship's railing.

Other shots rattled off in quick succession, and Chi-Kan knew he'd never heard anything like the turmoil of detonations. Once the pistols emptied, the fighting turned to cutlasses and knives.

Chi-Kan watched, frozen. He was no warrior, and he was no killer, either. A wet sob of pain from behind him caught his attention. When he turned, he saw Pak-Hong lying on the deck and grasping his bloody chest.

Pak-Hong coughed, and blood that looked black in the moonlight covered his lips.

Crossing the deck, Chi-Kan cradled the old man's head on his knees. "Pak-Hong! Pak-Hong!"

The old man looked up at Chi-Kan. He was already fading fast. "I didn't want to die a pirate," the old man gasped. He grabbed the younger man's hand. "Promise me that you won't die a pirate, too."

Tears burning at the back of his eyes, Chi-Kan nodded. "I promise."

"Remember, Chi-Kan, remember your promise," the old man gasped, grabbing Chi-Kan's hand with faltering strength. "Sometimes the evil a man does taints his blood and the blood of his children for generations to come. You don't just live for yourself. The gods hold us accountable for our actions for a long time." A long breath went out of Pak-Hong then, and his eyes stared off at nothing. His hand became limp, dropping from Chi-Kan's.

Running footsteps closed on Chi-Kan. Looking up, he spotted one of the ship's crew racing at him with a raised cutlass. Slowly, knowing the sailor meant to kill him and that there would be no one to care for his family if he died, Chi-Kan lifted the pistol and fired point-blank into the man's chest.

The ball caught the sailor high in the chest and knocked him back and down.

Chi-Kan shoved the useless pistol in his waist sash as he got to his feet. He raised his cutlass then and got ready to defend himself, wrapping himself in his anger and making it righteous. He wasn't going to die a pirate, but he wasn't going to live as a poor man, either. Whatever the ship held, part of the cargo was his. The profit from reselling the cargo would be enough to help his family. Mastering his resolve, he joined the battle and prayed that he wouldn't die and that the gods wouldn't turn against him.

New York City

Mack Bolan, aka the Executioner, drove through the congested noon traffic on Mott Street and kept his eyes on the target. Driving in Manhattan traffic was next to impossible without trying to keep up with someone else on the move. Tailing the target car on foot would have been easier in some areas, but that hadn't been an option and wouldn't have been in character with the ID he planned to play out. He'd been with the crew for the past twenty minutes, picking them up from the restaurant where Leo Turrin had told the Executioner he could find the men.

The six hardmen rode in a long black sedan that stood out in the Chinatown neighborhood. The men were there to make a statement, Bolan knew, and they wanted everyone to know who had made it when the dust settled.

The noise of Chinatown rolled in through Bolan's partially open window. Voices, horns and music all mixed together to make a cacophony. The smell of spices and foods pushed into the sedan, as well as the industrial stench of the city.

Brilliantly colored signs mounted on buildings or jutting from them, most of them red and yellow, held advertising in Chinese characters and English. Restaurants, jewelry shops, butcher shops, herb shops, clothiers and temples occupied the street on both sides. Five- and six-story buildings framed Mott Street, and some of them held the fat, bulbous shapes of water towers that shared roof space with advertising billboards and satellite dishes. Fire escape ladders made spidery scrawls up the sides of buildings. Thronging crowds filled the sidewalks, and pedestrians darted between the cars even when the lights weren't in their favor.

The target sedan turned abruptly and pulled into a parking garage next to a four-story building that housed a Chinese restaurant and laundry on the bottom floor. According to the intel that Turrin had passed along, the second and third floors were office rental space, the majority of it empty. Storage space claimed the fourth floor, but most of that was unoccupied, as well.

The office space rentals didn't turn a profit, and the laundry and restaurant broke even most months or showed a little profit. Still, the building turned a lot of money in gambling. Behind the ground-floor businesses was housed a major bookie operation that the NYPD Asian organized-crime units hadn't stumbled onto yet.

Bolan halted at the light, watching the mirrors as the big sedan's brake lights flared ruby in the shadows of the parking garage. Then the car slid on into the building.

Six men, Turrin had said, and he'd been certain they were being set up.

Glancing to his right, Bolan spotted an alley and steered into it. Potholes filled the alley, staggered between overflowing Dumpster garbage bins. Rotting vegetables and burned cooking grease tainted the air.

The Executioner pulled to a stop beneath a fire escape next to one of the large garbage bins. He got out of the car, leaving the air conditioner and moving into the heavy, oppressive breeze blowing listlessly through the alley. His combat senses flared to life, putting up the radar screen of personal protection that he'd first learned to use in the jungle half a world away.

"Hey, mister," a young voice called out.

Bolan looked up and spotted a half-dozen preteen children clinging to the fire escape. They shared the space with potted plants, lawn chairs, small Webber grills and laundry on hangers.

A small Asian boy of eleven or twelve stood. He was raw-boned and gangly, with flat eyes that had lost their innocence a long time ago. "If you leave your car there like that, somebody's going to come along and jack it, man."

Bolan gave the kid an easy grin, playing the part. "You think so?"

The boy nodded. "I know so. This is Green Ghost territory."

According to Bolan's intel, the Green Ghosts was the name of a young Chinese street gang that cooperated with the United Bamboo triad crime organization. The Executioner took a look at the sleek black Lexus SC-430 sport coupe. The car didn't mean anything to him and was only a tool that helped keep the identity he wore now.

Bolan looked back at the boy. "What do you think I should do?" His internal clock kept time, knowing he was still in the safe zone on the operation. But time always worked against a warrior in the long run.

"Hire somebody to look out for your car," the boy suggested.

"Who?"

"Me." The boy thumped his chest with a fist.

"You can protect my car?"

"Sure. But it'll cost you."

"How much?"

The boy thought for a moment. "One hundred dollars."

Bolan knew the boy was taking in the black suit he wore, as well as the wraparound sunglasses. Plus, Bolan was *fan kuei*. The term loosely translated into "foreign devil," an outsider. Outsiders were meant to be taken advantage of. That was a standard in most societies and had been since the dawn of the idea of community.

"Fifty dollars," Bolan countered, taking a bill from his wallet in his jacket pocket. He trapped the bill under the driver's-side wiper of the Lexus.

The boy hesitated only a moment. "Okay." Then he scrambled down through the fire escape, as lithe as a monkey. "I'll watch your car good."

Bolan nodded and left, walking out to the street and crossing in long strides. He glanced up at the building and saw the six men filing into the Chinese restaurant. As he threaded through the heavy pedestrian traffic along the sidewalk, the Executioner felt a hunter's eyes on him. He didn't look around even though he wondered who the player would ultimately turn out to be.

Bolan scanned the street for unmarked police cars. In the neighborhood, the vehicles would have stood out. Turrin's intel had indicated the NYPD and the FBI didn't know anything about the meeting going down today, but the situation could change at any moment.

The numbers on the op fell softly through Bolan's mind as he stepped into the restaurant. He scanned the dining area, all dressed out in red-and-black lacquer, with montages of dragons and warriors from Chinese mythology on the walls.

Artificial cherry blossoms occupied vases on the tables, flanked by long red candles. The lunch crowd took less than half the seats.

The six men the Executioner had followed in were nowhere in sight.

A young hostess in a white blouse and black skirt that hugged her slender curves greeted him. "Will you be dining with us?"

"Yes," Bolan said.

"Will anyone be joining you?"

"No."

The hostess smiled again and nodded. "This way, please." She tried to sit him near the front of the restaurant so he would have the view outside.

"I'd like to sit in the back," Bolan said.

"Of course." The hostess took him back, seated him and gave him the menu, taking time to pitch the buffet.

Bolan ordered the buffet and tea, then kept watch over the front door. He didn't have long to wait. As the hostess brought him the tea, three Chinese men strode through the door. The new arrivals wore casual dress, slacks, shirts and light jackets. They gave the appearance of businessmen or professionals, but Bolan picked up the shoulder rigs and belt holsters beneath the jackets. The tailoring was good, and would have hidden the presence of the weapons to all but the trained eye.

Bolan sipped his tea as the three men passed.

None of them talked as they made their way to the back of the restaurant. Obviously knowing they weren't there for the lunch buffet, the hostess didn't try to intercept them. They disappeared behind a folding screen.

Tossing his napkin onto the table, Bolan got up and walked toward the back of the restaurant.

The hostess hurried over to him.

"Bathroom?" Bolan asked, pointing to the back.

Uncertainly, the hostess nodded. "To the right."

"Thanks." Bolan went behind the folding screen and stepped through the door at the back of the restaurant. The bathroom doors were to the right, but a small cargo elevator was to the left.

The three Chinese men looked at Bolan, their faces immobile. The man in the rear opened the collapsible elevator cage door. The elevator walls held scars from scratches and cigarette burns. A naked lightbulb with a chain hung from the elevator's ceiling.

Without warning, pistol shots and shotgun blasts echoed down the elevator shaft, followed immediately by bursts of autofire.

Bolan didn't turn away, didn't act surprised or shocked. And that, he realized in the space of a heartbeat, was a mistake.

The three Chinese men grabbed under their jackets for their pistols.

Moving with lightning quickness, the Executioner reached under his jacket and stripped the pair of Beretta 93-Rs from the double jackass shoulder rig he wore. He pointed the weapons, acquiring his targets by instinct honed in countless battles. Bullets ripped the air over his head, smashed into the walls on either side of him, plucked at his jacket.

Bolan stroked the Beretta's triggers calmly, putting rounds into the heads of all three men. The 9 mm Parabellum slugs chewed through flesh and bone, crunched their skulls and drove the dead men backward. Blood covered the walls of the elevator cage.

The din of gunfire was followed immediately by hoarse shouts and screams of panic out in the dining room.

Listening to the sounds of battle still echoing down the elevator shaft, Bolan was in motion before the dead men hit the floor. He leathered his left pistol, then grabbed the jackets of the two dead men who had fallen inside the elevator cage and dragged them out.

Stepping inside the cage, Bolan pulled the door shut and glanced at the control panel. He pressed the button for the top floor, then changed out the partially used magazines in both pistols for fresh ones he carried in ammo pouches at the back of his belt.

The ancient elevator motor wheezed and chugged, lurching into motion, and the Executioner went up to the next battlefield. The six men he'd been tailing had stepped into a trap.

"WE'RE FUCKIN' dead here!"

Scared and certain that he'd just been told the truth, Joey Cimino pressed himself against the concrete support post where he and Tony the Mule had gone into hiding when it had all gone to hell.

"We're not dead," Cimino argued, but his voice broke and he didn't sound as convincing as he would have liked. He was twenty-five years old and had been an active enforcement arm for the De Luca Family in New York City for the past three years. The action in the storage area in Chinatown was the first serious firefight he'd ever been involved in. Until now, all he'd had to do was hang around and look tough.

"Maybe you figured a way out?" Tony the Mule challenged. He was a fat man and going bald, one of the old-school muscle guys who talked the talk and walked the walk. He was a guy who would hold the line and die if it came to that. Tony the Mule had been downtown and up the river, and was known as a stand-up guy.

"No," Cimino replied. He just didn't like the idea of thinking of himself as dead. But things weren't looking so good.

"I told Nick we should of found these fucks and whacked them somewheres else," Tony said. "Done 'em one at a time. You ask me, Nick's been watching too many movies. Fucker thought he was invincible."

Cimino had come to the building with Tony and the others to talk to the Russian *mafiya* soldiers they'd heard were in the area. They were supposed to talk to the guys and kind of poke around, ask a few questions for Don De Luca. With the kind of muscle the Don could put on the street, he had figured the *mafiya* guys would have been glad to talk to save their own asses.

The situation hadn't worked out that way. The Russians had pulled their pieces before Tony had three words out of his mouth. Of course, the fact that those first three words had been "You rat-fuck bastards" probably hadn't helped.

Now Nick and Ernie were on the floor and didn't look as if they would be getting back up. Blood seeped out of both men in growing pools, and neither moved.

Tony leaned around the support pole and fired the .357 hand cannon he carried. Bullets from the Russians' weapons, some of them fully automatic assault rifles, carved chunks from the pillar.

The don hadn't expected the Russians to go ballistic. Leo Turrin, a semiretired capo from the Five Families in New York, had advised De Luca things were going to get messy. He'd wanted the don to wait, but De Luca had ignored the advice.

And *we're going to pay the price,* Cimino thought. He peered around the pillar.

The top floor of the building was all storage space that hadn't been used in years. Rusted hulks of air-conditioning units, metals files, defunct restaurant equipment and boxes of surplus goods from past businesses that had occupied the offices below sat in abandoned clumps around the floor. Besides the dozen or so support pillars, there were also three long folding tables set up in a U-shape that supported computer equipment.

Cimino didn't know exactly what kind of business the Russians ran from the desolate building in the heart of Chinatown, although he guessed they might be there to handle overflow on bets the Chinese bookies operating below might want to lay off. But common sense told him that the don wouldn't have sent him there just for that. The don kept his own counsel, and if Nick Manetti had known, he hadn't told anyone else.

Wouldn't be telling anyone else, Cimino amended, looking at his uncle's body. Uncle Nick had brought him into the crew, going out of his way to make sure his nephew was a made guy in Family business.

The Russians had taken up positions throughout the other side of the storage area. They were behind the pillars and stacks of abandoned pallets. If the battle had just been against the four Russians they'd been told about, Cimino thought they might have been able to hold their own. But there were also the Chinese triad members who had stepped out of seclusion only moments ago, cutting off the retreat to the cargo elevator in the far corner. Cimino knew they were outnumbered three or four to one.

The Russians had set them up, drawn them in and were prepared to execute them.

They weren't dead yet, but a miracle had to happen before they walked out of there in one piece, Cimino thought. Bullets struck the pillar close to his head. Sparks leaped into the air and stone splinters raked his cheek with burning pain.

One of the Chinese triad members broke cover, throwing himself from behind an overturned three-compartment stainless-steel sink to close in on Cimino's position. An Uzi machine pistol rattled in his arms.

Heart hammering inside his chest, Cimino lifted the Colt .45 he carried. The pistol, one his father had carried before getting busted on a trafficking rap by the NYPD's Organized Crime Bureau, felt like an anvil at the end of his arm. He squeezed the trigger twice, putting both rounds in the center of his target and not going for a head shot because the chances of hitting a moving man's head were so small.

The rounds caught the Chinese in the chest, breaking his forward momentum, then robbing him of his motor control and dumping his corpse to the scarred concrete floor. He rolled amid the brass that had spilled from the Uzi, his eyes locked in a thousand-yard stare as a trickle of blood seeped from the corner of his mouth.

Cimino looked at the dead man, the first guy he'd ever killed. The Chinese guy looked younger than him.

Sickness twisted the young Mafia soldier's stomach. Sitting around listening to the old guys tell their stories from the old days, doing stuff like this had seemed glamorous, like day-to-day business. But the situation was different now because Cimino was convinced that he was going to end up on the warehouse floor just like the guy he'd put there.

"Kid," Tony the Mule growled, "don't you be fuckin' freezin' up on me. I need you to hold it together till we get outta here."

Cimino jerked his eyes from the dead Chinese gunner. He stared through the haze of gunsmoke that hung in the still air of the warehouse, listening to the growl of traffic in the street below. The war zone was an island, removed from the rest of the world.

Voices rang out in staccato Chinese, interspersed with Russian.

"Tony!" Pronzini yelled.

"Yeah."

"Where the hell's Nick?"

"Nick's got the shit shot out of him."

A scattered burst of gunfire halted the conversation for a moment. Cimino fired a pair of rounds at one of the Russians, the one with the ponytail.

"Somebody needs to call for backup," Pronzini yelled.

"No shit," Tony replied. "I got fifty cents if you got a phone handy."

"Nick's got a fuckin' phone," Pronzini protested.

"Nick's still got the fuckin' phone. And he don't look like he's gonna be callin' anybody."

Perspiration trickled down Cimino's face, but he kept the .45 up beside him, tracking the shadows that flitted through the warehouse and waiting for another shot. He hadn't brought a lot of ammunition, and they were definitely outclassed by the firepower the Chinese triad members had brought.

He glanced at Nick's body, thinking about the phone his uncle carried in the jacket pocket. Even if he could get the phone and could place the call, there was no guarantee that help would arrive in time.

Suddenly, the distinctive sound of a bullet tearing into flesh rang in Cimino's ears. For an instant, he thought Tony had been hit, then he realized his own leg was going out from under him, refusing to support his weight. He stared down at the dark blood that blossomed across his right pant leg.

He'd been shot. Panic set in, biting deeply into him and screaming inside his head.

Before Cimino could fall, Tony the Mule grabbed his jacket in one big ham-size fist.

"Hold on, kid," Tony snarled, pulling him back against the pillar.

Cimino rested against the pillar, sucking in a deep breath, feeling the pain moving in him now. He rested his weight on his good leg and felt the warmth of his blood cascading down his leg, watching the liquid pool on his shoe.

"Get ready," Tony said. "They smell the blood on us now. Here they come."

Glancing around the pillar, Cimino watched as the Chinese triad members closed ranks and upped their rate of fire, blowing hunks out of the pillar now as they flanked the two Mafia men. Bullets screamed from the hard surfaces. Tony blasted through his shots, drew back to safety, flipped the cylinder out of the .357 and dumped brass onto the floor before clicking another full load from a speed loader into his weapon.

Then the cargo elevator rose, the motor hardly making any noise at all in comparison to the gunfire. Smoke eddied around the elevator cage, and for a moment Cimino thought he only imagined the man in black cloaked in the shadows inside.

As the cargo elevator locked into position, the man in black stepped out. He stood a few inches over six feet, a big man built lean and hard. He wore a black suit over a black turtleneck, and black wraparound sunglasses masked his eyes. His hair was black and the jawline was granite, and there wasn't a moment of hesitation about him. Black pistols in both hands held extended magazines that thrust out past the butts.

A startled yell from one of the Chinese triad members drew the attention of the others. Evidently they hadn't been expecting anyone to flank them.

Then Cimino noted the crimson splashes on the inside of the elevator cage. Whoever the guy was, he'd bought into the attack in a big way.

The Chinese triad gunners turned toward the man in black,

but their bullets only ripped the air where he'd stood and drummed into the crimson-stained elevator cage. On the move, both pistols blazing and brass glistening in midair, the man in black cut a deep swath into the ranks of the Asian hardforce. Bodies toppled and dropped as rounds cored through their skulls and faces.

In three seconds, maybe less, seven triad members lay sprawled on the floor, taken out of the play.

Tony nudged Cimino, almost knocking the younger man from his feet when he put his weight on his injured leg.

"C'mon, kid. That guy ain't gonna make it on his own." He leaned out, and the distinct boom of the .357 cut through the sound of battle.

Cimino leaned around the pillar and added his firepower. The Chinese and the Russians had turned their attention away from the four surviving Mafia enforcers as they concentrated on the man in black who moved among them. Part of Cimino was hypnotized watching the deadly fighter's actions. The young mafioso had never seen anything like the man's movements. It was as if every step were choreographed, designed to move him just ahead of the enemy guns and into position to cut down his opponents.

As he struggled against the pain that filled him, Cimino's own rounds smashed against abandoned restaurant equipment and crates of unsold and discontinued sales goods.

The man in black cycled his pistols dry and stepped behind a stack of filing cabinets that had probably been made obsolete as businesses switched over to computer filing. Bullets tore through the thin sheet metal and left gaping holes in their wake.

Two triad gang members rushed the filing cabinets, their machine pistols yammering. Cimino fired at the running Chinese gunners but couldn't score a hit because his arm was shaking so much.

Just when he was certain the man in black didn't have a chance, the guy slid away from the filing cabinets on his side. Both hands were before him, the pistols recharged, muzzle-flashes erupting from the barrels. Bullets caught the two Chinese gunmen on the run, ripping into them and knocking them back. Before the dead men hit the floor, the man in black was up and running again.

Cimino reloaded, jamming his last magazine into his weapon.

"Who the fuck is this guy?" Pronzini yelled.

"Who cares?" Tony roared back. "He's killin' the guys that woulda killed us!" He threw the .357 forward and took another shot, hammering one of the Russian *mafiya* to the floor.

"Tony," the man in black called out, "I want the Russians left alive."

"Fuck you," Tony called back, pumping another round into the back of the downed Russian's skull. "These guys killed Nick. They're all goin' down."

The man in black slammed back against a wall and picked off a Chinese gunner who had taken the high ground atop a stack of crates. The triad guy dropped to the floor in a loose heap.

Just as the corpse hit the floor, the man in black swung his pistols on Tony. Bullets slammed against the concrete pillar. Cimino felt the impacts vibrate against his back.

"What the hell is that bastard doin'?" Tony yelped.

"He's making sure you don't kill any more Russians. I get the feeling that if you try, he's going to drop you."

"Who the fuck does this guy think he is?"

"Right now," Cimino said, "he's the guy saving our asses." He worked his reload and glanced back at the battlefield, but he couldn't see the man in black anywhere.

2

Silence hung heavy and oppressive in the fourth-floor storage area.

Mack Bolan stood with his shoulders pressed against a wall of crates, the positions of the four mafiosi marked in his mind. From what he'd gathered, three of the Russians and two Chinese triad members remained alive. All of them were up and moving.

"Tony," Bolan called, knowing his voice was going to be bait for the killers around him.

"Yeah?"

"Don De Luca wants the Russians left alive, too."

"How the fuck am I supposed to know that? I got my orders. They said come here, whack the goddamn Commies and call it a day. I don't know you from Adam."

The wall of sound coming from the open windows along the east side quieted for a split second. The silence was just enough to let Bolan know a body had passed between the windows and him. He wheeled instantly and thrust both Berettas before him, catching the triad gangster in midstride.

The gangster tried to bring up his machine pistol, yanking the trigger and stuttering a line of ragged fire across the concrete floor.

The Executioner squeezed a triburst from each of the 93-Rs. Hollowpoint rounds crashed through the gangster's chest and drove him backward. Bolan remained in motion, already around the line of crates before the spinning brass hit the floor.

"How do I know you ain't here to help the Russians outta this?" Tony demanded.

"They were out of here," Bolan declared. "You were dead before I got here." He scanned the aisle between the crates.

Sirens ripped through the city noises in the distance and got steadily closer.

"Look," a man said with a Baltic accent from Bolan's left, "maybe we can all get out of here alive. *Da?*"

"I was sent down here to give you fucks a message," Tony said. "Stay outta Family business in our neighborhood. You guys are supposed to be the message." He raised his voice. "An' they're supposed to be dead, wiseguy."

"Not anymore," Bolan said.

"I don't answer to you," Tony argued. "Don De Luca, he gives me orders."

"Kill another one of the Russians," Bolan warned, "and you'll earn a toe tag." He kept moving, his combat senses alert.

At the end of the aisle of crates, a man stepped out into Bolan's path. The Executioner checked his immediate impulse to fire, seeing that the man was European, not Asian. Bolan dropped and threw himself forward in a baseball slide, feeling the heat from the bullet that barely missed him, hearing the thunderclap an instant later.

The man went down when Bolan cut his knees from beneath him. The Russian landed hard, his eyes wide with fear, just able to catch himself on one arm. He lifted his arm and tried to shove his pistol into Bolan's face.

The Executioner whipped his left arm around and caught the man in the side of the face with the Beretta 93-R. The man's eyes rolled upward and he relaxed on the floor. Bolan pushed himself to his feet, listening to the sound of running feet ahead. Turning effortlessly, he pursued the running man, glancing through gaps in the crates to see another Russian trying an end run around the crates to get to the cargo elevator. The Executioner reached the other end of the aisle before the fleeing man.

The man approached at a dead run, his breath rasping through his open mouth. Bolan gauged the man's arrival, set himself, threw out an elbow that caught the guy in the throat, spinning with the impact.

The Russian was a couple of inches shorter than Bolan, and heavier by a hundred pounds, but he was staggered, his throat paralyzed. He was reaching for his neck, gasping for breath, when the Executioner rapped him on the forehead with the pistol butt and put him to sleep.

Catching motion in his peripheral vision, Bolan spun back toward the crates. Autofire hammered the side of the crates above the unconscious Russian, driving wooden splinters into the air. Having no choice, knowing the Chinese gangster was the last one left, Bolan leathered the Beretta he grasped in his left hand, found a handhold and a foothold in the crates and climbed.

"Is that guy still alive?" one of the mafiosi asked.

"Don't know," a younger man's voice replied. "I lost him."

"Can't be anybody left."

"If the guy in black isn't around," the younger man insisted, "then somebody got him. Do the math, Pronzini."

Pronzini swore.

Bolan gained the top of the stack and went prone on the dust-covered tarp draped over the top layer of crates. He glanced down and saw the final triad gangster easing around the corner of the stack at the end of the aisle where he'd gone up.

Dust floated down from the tarp. Scattering the debris had been unavoidable as Bolan had claimed the high ground. The Chinese gunner stepped into the descending dust cloud and sneezed. Realization of what had caused the dust cloud jerked his head up, the machine pistol following, stitching a line of bullets up the side of the crates.

Extending his arm over the side of the crate as the bullets chopped up at him, the Executioner took deliberate aim and squeezed the trigger. The 9 mm Parabellum slugs slapped into the bridge of the gangster's nose between his eyes and snapped his head back.

The Chinese gangster took two stumbling steps backward, dropping the machine pistol, then sat down heavily. A moment later, his body slumped over sideways.

Bolan reloaded both his weapons but kept only the one in his right hand as he stood and surveyed the area. No one looked up, and no one noticed him. He spotted the two dead Mafia hardguys from Don De Luca's camp. Two more, one he recognized as Tony the Mule from the OCB pictures Leo Turrin had sent, took shelter behind one of the support pillars. Another Mafia enforcer was hiding behind a three-compartment sink while the sixth hid behind a stack of crates.

The remaining Russian broke cover from the hulk of a rusting HVAC unit, streaking for the cargo elevator. He was tall and lean, wearing a full beard, a ponytail and hoop earrings, and was clad in a steel-gray designer suit.

Bolan took two running strides down the stack of crates and dropped ten feet to the floor. He pushed off at once, knowing the Russian was in Tony the Mule's line of fire. Driving his feet hard, Bolan cut down the ground between himself and his quarry. From the corner of his eye, he spotted Tony the Mule swinging around the corner, a stainless-steel .357 Magnum pistol thrust out before him.

The Executioner threw himself forward just as the Russian heard him coming and turned around. The Russian's eyes narrowed as he brought up an H&K .40-caliber pistol.

Bolan fired on the fly, slamming a bullet into the Russian's shoulder, knocking the man off balance. The Executioner left his own feet, catching the Russian from the side and throwing them both wide of the cargo elevator as Tony the Mule's fusillade hammered the gaping doorway.

The Russian groaned as he hit the concrete floor, and the H&K flew from his hand.

Straddling the Russian's chest, Bolan fisted the man's shirt and levered his forearm against his captive's throat, choking him down.

His voice as cold as the graveyard, the Executioner screwed the Beretta's muzzle into the Russian's left cheekbone and said, "Live or die."

Stilling instantly, the Russian pulled his arm back. Pain contorted his face. "*Da,*" he croaked around the arm pressed into his throat. "Live. I want to live."

"Good," Bolan growled.

Running footsteps sounded behind the Executioner. Maintaining his hold on his prisoner, he turned and lifted the Beretta into target acquisition as he stared back at Tony the Mule across the .357's barrel. Bolan wore a lightweight

Kevlar vest beneath the suit jacket. Though the body armor would guarantee no bullet would penetrate, the blunt trauma would leave him bruised and hurting for days.

"Get away from him," Tony commanded as he held the .357 in a double-fisted grip.

"No," Bolan replied. "I'm pulling rank here, Tony."

"Pullin' rank?" Confusion creased the big mafioso's face. "What the fuck're you talkin' about?"

Slowly Bolan reached into the breast pocket of his jacket. He took a card out with two fingers, then flicked it forward.

The card spun through the air and landed on the concrete between them face up.

"The ace of spades," said the injured young man beside Tony the Mule. He raised his eyes, now filled with awe and wonderment rather than pain, and gazed at Bolan. "Tony, he's a Black Ace, man."

A Black Ace was the crème de la crème among the Italian Mafia—enforcers with the power from La Commissione to take out a capo, a boss in the Family. No one questioned a Black Ace and lived. Black Aces walked above most Family business, and only worked on things for the good of all the Families. Usually when a Black Ace showed up, somebody died.

The role of a Black Ace was one Bolan had played before.

The Executioner stared up at Tony the Mule, keeping the big man's face squarely in his sights. "So, Tony, what's it going to be?"

The big man's eyes returned to the black ace of spades on the concrete. He lowered the .357 Magnum.

"Good," Bolan said, listening to the scream of approaching sirens.

STANDING IN THE BREEZEWAY of the small building owned by her family business, Saengkeo Zhao stared out at the tiny playground where her nephews, nieces and cousins played on swings and jungle gyms. A smile dawned in her heart and wouldn't rest until the feeling touched her lips, as well.

The children lived for the times they could be free from their schoolwork and from the regimentation of the classroom. And Saengkeo felt at times as though she lived for the precious moments she could spend watching the children. There were fewer of those moments these days, and even the sound of the children's laughter sometimes failed to draw her from the darkness of her thoughts.

She stood straight and tall, wearing a patchwork kimono jacket featuring blues, greens and a splash of rust over a black necklace top and pearlized, slim-fit black leather pants. Supple Italian shoes encased her feet, and she'd deliberately stayed away from high heels, preferring comfort and sure-footedness. She wore her black hair cut short, squared off with her chin and tapered to her head. Her dress was Western, and she knew some of the people she would be seeing that morning would be offended by her choice. But the clothing felt comfortable and suited her.

"Saengkeo."

Turning from the children, Saengkeo faced Ea-Han. "Uncle," she said politely.

The old man nodded and smiled, standing with some effort as he clutched his cane with trembling hands for support. He was in his eighties, she knew, but how old exactly he would never say, nor would he permit himself to be asked without delivering a scathing rebuke.

His silver hair was long and wispy, matching the thin strings of his mustache and beard sprouting from his pointed chin. His hands were thin, veins bulging on the backs of them like feeding leeches, fingers thin and brown and curled around the cane handle like dried sticks. He wore a white robe and black pants.

"You did not tell me you were coming this morning, daughter," the old man said.

Ever since Saengkeo could remember, even when her parents had been alive, Ea-Han had called her his daughter. The old man had been employed on one of her father's fishing boats then, and he had been the one to teach her to fish while her father tended the family business. Her mother had stayed in the family house, taking care of the things there. Saengkeo had been destined for such duties, as well, but her father had relented—spoiled her, according to her mother—and Saengkeo had been given the opportunity to experience more of the world than most female children who grew up in the Aberdeen Harbour area on the south side of Hong Kong Island.

"In truth, Uncle," Saengkeo said, walking toward the old man, "I didn't know I was coming here until I was parked out front." Her troubled thoughts had drawn her to the building, and to the children. She had worked there when she was younger, and had gone to school there before that.

"You picked a good time," Ea-Han said. "I know how much you like to watch the children at play, and they've not yet been called in to morning class."

"Seeing them pleases me greatly." She took hold of the old man's arm, feeling his lack of strength and the way he trembled.

"There was a time," Ea-Han said, "when you knew all their names."

"I still do."

"Perhaps," he stated. "But there was also a time when all the children knew you. Now they only know your name and that you are someone they should treat with respect. I miss those days, daughter."

"As do I, Uncle."

Gently Saengkeo guided the old man back to the small stone bench she'd ordered built in the shade of a parasol tree near the children's school area. With the constant climate permitted by the harbor area and the proximity of the sea, the parasol tree remained covered in leaves that measured almost a foot across. Still, there were many new leaf clusters in sight.

"I am glad that you found time in your busy day to visit us," Ea-Han said, easing himself onto the padded UCLA bench seat that he'd received as a gift from her. She'd sent him the bench seat from her college days abroad, another facet of her life that her mother had found appalling. But her father had allowed her to study in the United States and other countries. "You've been too long gone from us."

"Our business grows complicated these days, Uncle," Saengkeo replied. Guilt chafed at her.

"As do all businesses," Ea-Han said. "But I trust you, daughter. All of the family trusts you when it comes to making the right decisions as to how we are to proceed. Your father trusted you. That's why he let you wander so far from us for so long."

Saengkeo watched the children at play, squealing and laughing, and wondered if her father had ever thought that she might one day be the head of the family and be making decisions about the family business. No one could have seen that, she told herself. She hadn't seen the day coming, hadn't guessed that an unknown enemy would assassinate her brother, Syn-Tek, months ago.

Tears burned the backs of her eyes, but she refused to shed them. She would cry in her own time, as she always had.

"This is going to be a beautiful day," Ea-Han stated.

Gazing up at the clear blue sky with the rosy dawn still

hanging in the eastern skies, Saengkeo agreed. Tall sky-scrapers, some of them housing internationally based busi-nesses and some of them the Chinese government temporary housing high-rises called estates, spiked the skyline. Two helicopters marked in a popular tourist company's colors drifted through the tall city like dragonflies looking for a promising cattail.

"Yes," Saengkeo agreed. She tried not to see the high cin-der-block security wall around the children's play area that cut them off from the neighborhood. Artists had painted the inside of the wall, peppering it with favorite cartoon charac-ters from the United States, Japan and China. Access to satel-lite television made all the characters known to the children.

The wall was there for a reason. This day while she looked at the cinder-block wall topped with razor wire, she feared that the wall wasn't enough. The enemies of her family were gathering like sharks that smelled blood in the water.

Three young women wearing black schoolteacher robes with white collars watched over the children. A fourth one strode from the building and down the stone walkway be-tween landscaped garden spots containing flowering bushes. The new teacher took a metallic-blue whistle from her skirt pocket.

"No," Ea-Han called out in his reedy voice.

The schoolteacher glanced at the old man with a little an-noyance.

Ea-Han waved a trembling hand at the teacher, dismiss-ing her. "The children can play a few more minutes today."

The woman bowed her head and walked back into the building. Ea-Han had been made director of the school four-teen years ago at Saengkeo's insistence. She had been twenty then, in school at UCLA in California, and had commanded her father's ear in some matters.

"When the children learn that they received more time from you for playing today," Saengkeo said with a smile, "you'll be their hero."

The old man leaned in conspiratorially. "Actually, daughter, I am their hero most days. When they see me out here on this bench, when I have the strength to make it out this far, they know they will get extra time in the playground. Strong minds in strong bodies. They should have the best of both worlds."

Saengkeo silently agreed. Her great-grandfather, Jik-Chang Zhao, had first conceived of the school while still in Shanghai, then had moved the school to Hong Kong Island when the family business took them there. In those days, the school had only been for the boys while the girls stayed home and helped their mothers care for the house. Her father had opened the school to girls, but the families still maintained the right to send them or not. As things were, boys still outnumbered girls in the school by a margin of three to one.

"You are troubled, daughter," Ea-Han declared.

"Yes," she replied.

"Syn-Tek's death doesn't rest well on your mind."

"He was murdered, Uncle," Saengkeo said in a voice that was soft and distant from her, from the pain she didn't allow herself to feel. "His death will never rest easy on my mind."

"I have lost three brothers and two sisters," Ea-Han said. "I watched them die when the Japanese took Nanking during World War II. My father died also, but my mother escaped with me and we lived."

"I didn't know that," Saengkeo said.

"We have never spoken of the matter. There was no need before today."

"I'm sorry. I did not mean for my own sadness to trouble you with yours."

"My sadness no longer troubles me," Ea-Han said. "My life has moved on. As will yours."

"I pray that it will, Uncle."

"Yet you prepare yourself to find Syn-Tek's murderer."

Saengkeo didn't bother to deny the accusation.

"You would be better served," Ea-Han said, "to keep your eyes on the things that you need to do. Your heart and your head would remain clear."

"Someone murdered Syn-Tek," Saengkeo said.

"An army murdered my family," the old man replied. "I would have had to wipe out the Japanese army to feel better about my life if I'd remained as focused on being sad and unhappy as you are."

"I want revenge, Uncle."

"That is a Western thought, daughter. Buddha teaches us acceptance in the way things have to be, and asks that we pray for the strength to change the things that don't have to be."

"Syn-Tek was betrayed by someone close to him," Saengkeo said. "That's the only way he could have been killed."

Ea-Han was silent for a moment. "If you seek out that person or persons, your life may be forfeit, as well."

"No."

"You can't say that, daughter."

I can, Saengkeo thought. I will. But she didn't say those things out loud. She'd never argued with the old man, and she wasn't about to start now.

"Your wish," Ea-Han said, "and that of your brother and your father before you, and even to your grandfather, was that this family get away from the stain left by the pirate Chi-Kan Zhao when he took to criminal ways."

"I know." During the fifty-odd years following World War II when opportunity again presented itself, her father, followed by her brother, had worked to get their family out of triad business. They had several legitimate businesses going now, though all of them were small, mostly fishing boats and manufacturing plants. They had sacrificed profit for legitimacy, and that had made them weak in the eyes of some of the triads.

"Yet you will not put this matter from your heart."

"I can't." Saengkeo had been to place fresh flowers on her brother's grave that morning. "I miss him, Uncle. I miss Syn-Tek and the way he was. His children and his wife miss him."

"I know, daughter. But this is one of those things that must be accepted."

"I will try," Saengkeo replied, and it was the first time she'd ever lied to him. She wondered if he knew.

"Where are you going?" the old man asked.

"I have a meeting."

"With the other triad families?"

"Yes."

Ea-Han was silent for a short time. "You must be very careful, daughter. None of those men like having a woman in their midst."

"After Syn-Tek was killed, no one else could have run the family business," Saengkeo said. "There are other men in this family who have had to deal with that."

"Yes." Ea-Han nodded.

Saengkeo glanced at her watch and saw that it was a quarter to eight. Her meeting was scheduled for 2:00 p.m., and she wanted to arrive early.

"I must go, Uncle," Saengkeo said, getting up from the stone bench. "And you have to let the children go to their morning classes."

"I will," the old man said, "when it suits me. They are given more school and work than many other children in Hong Kong."

"Only because we want more from them than other children," Saengkeo said. "So they can want more from themselves."

"Go then, daughter, and I will pray for peace to touch your heart."

Saengkeo left the old man and the happy squeals of the children. She walked past the teachers gathered at the double doors leading to the building.

The teachers glanced at her nervously. All of them knew they were expected to teach the children so they could do more than their parents and grandparents before them. For more than two hundred years, the Zhao family had been involved in organized crime. They had been trying to escape that lifestyle, and had started reaping some of the success of those efforts.

Escape, however, wasn't going to be easily won. Taking care of a family, especially an extended one like the Moon Shadow triad, which had grown so large and so dependent on the money that crime paid, was expensive and consuming. Saengkeo knew firsthand because she had helped her father, then her brother make the necessary moves. The family had been undertaking more and more legitimate business ventures, losing some income to work within the law.

Then the British had returned Hong Kong to Communist Chinese rule in 1997. The resulting stock losses and setbacks had seriously damaged what Syn-Tek and Saengkeo had managed to work out. In the end, as her brother had explained it to her, there'd been no choice about doing some of the things he'd done. His actions had served to get them in territorial conflicts with some of the other triads.

The parking lot in front of the Moon Shadow family building was small. Few drivers stopped there. Saengkeo looked up at the ten-story building. The structure was white, like nearly all of the government-sponsored housing that had gone up since 1953 when a huge fire had left fifty thousand squatters without homes. At that time, the government had been left with no choice except to create a place to house those people.

Conventional housing projects consisted of seven or eight apartment buildings in a cluster. The cluster of buildings was called an estate, and contained schools, shopping centers and entertainment areas like gyms. Each thirty-story building held a thousand apartments and housed a population of three thousand to four thousand residents. The apartments were small, no more than 250 square feet, but they were better than squatting in huts or living on the streets as the residents had until the time the buildings had been erected.

A large number of squatters still remained in Hong Kong. Those people lived in ramshackle huts along the undeveloped harbor line and in alleys between businesses, warehouses and the tourist areas in Central downtown.

The unit that housed the Moon Shadow triad had been built to service squatters who had lived along the harbor. People who built ramshackle huts along the water's edge so they could fish and get by on what little income they could generate posed fire hazards to the cargo ships and dredging crews that constantly worked to improve the harbor for shipping and tourist trade.

Saengkeo's father had purchased the building back in the late 1960s and began pulling his family together, working to fulfill the promise their ancestor had sworn to back in the 1920s.

The sound of rubber whirring across the paved street drew Saengkeo's attention. Cars sped along the street, reminding her she had places to be, as well.

She turned and headed for the vintage and fully restored silver Mercedes 450 SL, keying the electronic ignition and the door locks in quick succession. She opened the door, took off her jacket and slid behind the wheel.

Shoving the stick into Reverse, Saengkeo let out the clutch and rolled backward. Pausing to wait for a break in the early-morning traffic, she reached into the glove compartment and took out a double shoulder holster rig containing a matched pair of matte-black Walther Model P-990 QPQs chambered in .40 S&W.

She had carried weapons like them for the past twenty years, since she was fourteen years old and her father feared he couldn't adequately protect her. He had even arranged for her to have gun permits while living abroad. The weapons had saved her life on occasion, and saved the lives of others. But she never wore them inside the school area of the building where the children were.

As she drove, Saengkeo shrugged into the shoulder holster with practiced ease, shrugged back into her kimono jacket, and ran a hand through her hair. She glanced at herself in the rearview mirror and remembered her mother's dissatisfaction with her daughter's vanity, insisting that she had learned it from the American television. Saengkeo's father had argued that his daughter needed to know Western ways and Western talk if she was going to help them save their family. Her father's decision to include her had sparked a number of family arguments. That had been when there were three of them, her father and her brother and her, to plan the acquisition of profitable businesses.

Now only she remained. And if her enemies killed her, no one would be left to finish saving their family.

While checking her reflection in the mirror, Saengkeo spotted the luxury stretch limousine that slid behind her. Her cell phone beeped at her, and she took the handset up from the console.

"Hello," Saengkeo said.

"Good morning, Saengkeo," a man's voice greeted cheerily.

Saengkeo glared at the image of the limousine in her rearview mirror, feeling panic and anger rise at the same time. But she kept her voice calm. "Good morning, Mr. Yang."

Wai-Lim Yang was head of the Black Swan gang, which was affiliated with both the Big Circle Society and United Bamboo. Yang sometimes operated as go-between for the two triads when their interests conflicted, and helped both groups save face so war wouldn't erupt in the streets in cities around the world where both groups conducted business. Tong wars had happened in the past and had proved costly to all concerned. That was why An-Koa Cao, one of the United Bamboo's lieutenants, was heading up the meeting later that day.

"I thought we might talk this morning," Yang said.

"A meeting has already been scheduled to discuss our differences," Saengkeo replied. She scanned the traffic, knowing Yang wouldn't follow her by himself. Of course, Yang might not even be in the limousine and the vehicle was only there to intimidate her. "It would be most unfortunate if you were to miss that meeting."

"I won't miss the meeting," Yang promised. "But there are things we need to discuss privately before that meeting."

"About how I should support your claim against Lo-Fat Ma's floating brothels?" Saengkeo shook her head. "No. He was there first. You already know how I feel about that."

"Perhaps you'll change your mind," Yang suggested in a soft voice. "I have information about Pei-Ling Bao."

Saengkeo felt a chill ghost through her. Pei-Ling Bao was a friend. They had grown up together at the Moon Shadow building, gone to school together and they'd remained friends even when Saengkeo had left Hong Kong for a time. But Pei-Ling had become a prostitute like her mother before her. Only Pei-Ling hadn't stayed a common streetwalker or someone who sold her body to tourists from one of the flower boats out in the harbor. She had become an expensive courtesan able to charge four figures a night. Despite Saengkeo's disapproval—and Pei-Ling had never been one to seek that approval—Pei-Ling had continued her work.

Six days ago, without a word, without a clue, Pei-Ling had disappeared from the face of the earth as if she'd never existed.

"What information?" Saengkeo demanded. She was no longer able to keep the emotion from her voice. Was Pei-Ling alive or dead? Her mother had asked Saengkeo that every day.

"I know where Pei-Ling is," Yang stated.

"Where?"

"We need to meet," Yang insisted. "We can work out a trade."

Saengkeo thought quickly. She knew Hong Kong Island and all of Kowloon along the mainland. What she wanted was a public place where Yang would be hesitant to resort to violence, as he usually did when he didn't get what he wanted.

"Meet me in Central," she told him. "In the open piazza in Exchange Square. In an hour."

"As you wish," Yang agreed.

"One other thing."

"What?"

"I want to know if Pei-Ling is alive." Saengkeo pushed her emotions away as she'd trained herself to do. In order to do any good at all for Pei-Ling, and for her family, she had to remain strong.

Still, memories of Pei-Ling playing in the playground Saengkeo had just left paraded through her mind. They'd promised to always be close, but Saengkeo felt that she hadn't been as good a friend as she had promised. Life and her family's business had gotten in the way.

Yang's voice mocked Saengkeo. "Only moments ago," the Black Swan crime boss said, "your main question was where your friend might be. You can wait a little longer for the rest."

The phone clicked dead.

Saengkeo's mind raced, sifting through the courses of action she had open to her. Stoddard, she knew, would be furious with her if she called him. So she didn't. Instead, she punched Johnny Kwan's number and pressed her foot harder on the accelerator, weaving through the traffic effortlessly and leaving the luxury limousine behind.

Things were coming to a head even sooner than she had believed they would.

New York City

Mack Bolan stood at the one-way glass and peered in at the prisoner. The Russian paced the small cinder-block room restlessly, gazing contemptuously at the one-way glass and the door. The room contained no furniture, had no window and was soundproofed.

Even standing in the observation room on the other side of the one-way glass, Bolan couldn't hear any of the night noises as nocturnal Manhattan came alive above them. He glanced at his watch and found it was 7:32 p.m.

Almost eight hours had passed since the Russians had been captured in Chinatown. All of them had been locked down since that time, hidden away in the basement dungeon Don De Luca had inherited from past crime bosses. A large drain occupied the slightly sloped tile floor. Tile covered the walls and ceiling, as well, except for the water nozzle jutting from the wall opposite the door.

In the fifties and sixties, Bolan knew, the place had probably been used for gangland executions. People had been brought to the rooms, killed brutally and painfully, and the bodies had been disposed of. Bolan was pretty sure the Russian knew that was what the room had been used for.

The door opened, drawing Bolan's attention. The Executioner turned smoothly, squaring himself up with the entrance. The chance existed that the Russian *mafiya* would come looking for its missing members.

Leo Turrin entered, carrying two white paper bags. The stocky little Fed was showing more gray these days, but he'd earned it. As a rising crime boss in the Mafia and an undercover officer working for the Justice Department's Organized Crime Task Force, he'd walked a tightrope between life and death for years. In the end, Turrin had hung up the game, living as a semiretired made man and occasionally helping out Hal Brognola's Sensitive Operations Group.

Unlike the cell on the other side of the one-way glass, the observation room held a small folding table and a half-dozen folding chairs. Turrin put his bags on the table next to a laptop and digital camera, and unfolded a chair.

"How's your guy doing?" Turrin nodded at the long-haired Russian.

"He's ready," Bolan answered.

Turrin took out two foam cups of coffee and passed one over, keeping the other for himself. "You going to talk to him?"

"When he's readier," Bolan said.

"I thought you had a time frame on this op."

"Ticking clock," Bolan said.

"How many ticks you get?"

Bolan shrugged. "Don't know yet."

"I've talked to Hal," Turrin said, "and I've talked to you. Both of you have been tight-lipped about what this is all about."

"The Russian downsizing that's still going on." Bolan cracked the cover over the cup and let the steam escape. "Seven weeks ago, an oil freighter sailed out of Magadan, Russia, and across the Sea of Okhotsk in the Russian far east. The freighter was carrying three cruise missile warheads that were supposed to be destroyed. Magadan has become a hotbed of investment interests. Besides oil and gas and engineering money that will be made, estimates say there's a billion dollars in gold in the area."

"A Russian gold rush?" Turrin grinned.

"That's what they say."

"Maybe it's time to break out the old parka and a mining pick."

Despite the tension of the operation and the long hours he'd already put in on the mission, Bolan smiled. Even when they were at death's door and expecting never to see another dawn, their friendship had always maintained humor.

The Russian banged on the door, swearing in English and Russian.

"Who had the warheads?" Turrin asked.

"The Russian Mob," Bolan replied. "A guy named Kasatka Bykov. The four guys that De Luca's people had holed up are soldiers for Bykov."

"You IDed them?" Turrin had been busy keeping everything smooth with Don De Luca. There had been several repercussions after the battle in Chinatown, more of them relating to keeping a lid on Family business that might be hit in retaliation by the triads than problems with the police.

Bolan nodded toward the laptop and digital computer. "Kurtzman did after I sent him a picture."

Aaron Kurtzman was Stony Man Farm's cybernetics wizard. Seated at his console in the Farm's Computer Room, he prowled the world's information systems.

Turrin pointed toward the long-haired Russian kicking the door. The dulled thumps barely invaded the observation room. "So who's this guy?"

"Pribik Askenov. He's been in New York longer than the three men he was with."

"The other three are all hardguys and shooters," Turrin said.

"Yeah. Askenov was the point guy for the meet with the Green Ghosts. He's an ex-KGB intelligence officer and speaks Cantonese and Mandarin."

Askenov kicked the door a final time, then turned and walked away in defeat and disgust. He sat against the far wall with his forearms resting on his knees, his head resting on his arms.

"And when I forwarded the intel that De Luca was fielding a team to whack a group of Russians trying to sell nuclear warheads here in Manhattan, Hal called you."

"Got it in one," Bolan agreed.

"I thought it was just a rumor," Turrin said. "But after September 11, I didn't want to take any chances."

"Yeah. Hal didn't see that Russians would be in the market to sell nuclear warheads they didn't have, though."

Turrin's eyes narrowed, showing he was tracking the situation. "If the Russians weren't there to sell nukes, that leaves them in the buying position."

"Yeah."

"And the triad has nukes for sale?"

"That's the big question," Bolan said.

"You never said who took down the Russian freighter."

"Chinese pirates," Bolan answered. "That's according to a CIA deep-cover agent in Hong Kong."

"No shit," Turrin replied. "Has Stony Man got a buy-in on this one?"

Bolan shook his head. "So far there's been no confirmation that the Green Ghosts have the warheads."

"Do they have a pirate arm of the organization?"

"They're part of the Big Circle Society," Bolan replied, gazing at the Russian. "The Big Circle has an arm for everything."

"So if we can find out that the Green Ghosts know where the nukes are, Hal turns Phoenix Force, Able Team and you onto them?"

Bolan shook his head. "Not yet. The CIA is all over this one. They've got a big covert op under way in China, but I don't have any information about that. Neither does Hal. So far, the Man is keeping us clear of the situation, leaving the search to the CIA."

Turrin grinned. "But you're buying into the pot on your own."

Bolan nodded. Being able to call his own shots was why he'd stepped away from and kept Stony Man Farm at arm's length. He was there when they needed him, but he developed things on his own, as well.

"I'm just peeking in," the Executioner said, "to keep the table honest."

Turrin sipped his coffee and looked into the holding cell. "We need something to break with your playmate in that room. I know you're using the time to let Askenov take himself apart, but it's not wearing any better on De Luca."

"De Luca's getting antsy?" Bolan knew that Turrin had exerted a lot of pressure and called in a lot of favors to back the mysterious Black Ace who had arrived like an avenging angel in Chinatown earlier that day. Saving the four Mafia enforcers from certain death at the hands of the Green Ghosts had helped.

Turrin grimaced. "De Luca sees himself as a patriot, Sarge.

After September 11 and the shakeup in the economy, De Luca is ready to turn a couple of gorillas with baseball bats loose in that cell. Askenov could talk or die, and De Luca believes it would be the guy's choice."

Tony the Mule or another old-line enforcer could probably have gotten the information that way, but Bolan didn't operate in that fashion. Unless all else failed.

"The Mafia has been steadily going more and more legit, and they've heavily invested in the stock market to do it. When the stocks crashed after the World Trade Center went down, they lost their shirts like a lot of other people. They don't want something like that to happen again." He paused. "Plus, they don't much care for the idea of the old neighborhood becoming a radioactive pit. I can't say that I blame them."

Bolan put down his empty coffee container. "Let's go talk to our guy."

Kowloon

"SO, HAVE YOU TRIED to get her into bed yet?"

Rance Stoddard came awake in a rush the way he always did when he was working in a hostile foreign country. For the past sixteen years, that had been most of his life. He craned his head over on the bed and spotted Jacy Corbin seated naked at the small desk in the hotel suite's bedroom.

Jacy was in her midtwenties, a hard-bodied blonde with long hair that trailed past her shoulder blades. She sat unladylike, one foot on the chair and knee bent to rest her arm as she smoked. Pale blond curls framed the triangle at the juncture of her thighs. This day her eyes were intense blue, but she changed contacts so often that Stoddard could no longer remember what color they actually were.

"What?" Stoddard asked.

"Have you tried to get her into bed yet?"

"Who?"

"Saengkeo Zhao," Corbin said.

"No."

"Ever dream about it? I mean, she's got that whole exotic Oriental whammy thing going on. And she's the head of her own crime cartel. Your golden girl."

Reluctantly Stoddard sat up. He knew from experience that when Jacy got one of her moods going she couldn't be stopped. "No," he answered. "I don't dream about getting her in bed."

Corbin took another hit on her cigarette and blew smoke at the ceiling. "Liar."

Stoddard gave her a disparaging look.

"You talk in your sleep," Corbin explained. "We have sex, you go to sleep and you dream. When you dream, you talk."

"If I start revealing any state secrets," Stoddard said, "you have my permission to shoot me."

Corbin grinned. "Okay, you don't talk about state secrets."

"I don't talk about sex with the Zhao woman, either," Stoddard growled. He levered himself out of bed and padded into the large, ornate bathroom.

"You do talk about her."

"No, I don't."

"Yes, you do," Corbin stated. "Maybe it's because she's more your age."

Stoddard was thirty-nine and worked out every day. He stood six feet four inches tall and had the same waist size he'd had as a football halfback in high school and college. He ran his hands through his dark auburn hair, kept high and tight in a military cut.

The Central Intelligence Agency advised several of its male agents operating in Asian, South American and African theaters not to wear their hair too short because they would be immediately identified as American military. Not that such identification would blow whatever covert op the agent was working on, but such an identification might prove life-threatening if a kidnapper decided to take the agent and try to ransom him to the United States military.

Most everything Stoddard had worked on as a CIA agent in the past ten years had come with a total disavowal. If he was caught by an enemy or discovered by a foreign government, he wouldn't be acknowledged or rescued.

Living on the edge like that was something Stoddard had learned to crave.

"Do you think maybe that's it?" Corbin persisted.

Stoddard took out his toiletry kit. Even after weeks of living at the expensive hotel in Kowloon, he hadn't unpacked the kit, keeping ready to move in a moment's notice if he had the chance to return to the hotel first. He put paste on his toothbrush and started brushing, glancing up in the mirror to see Jacy standing in the doorway, one lean, rounded haunch cocked against the frame.

"Her age?" Corbin pressed. "Do you think that's why you dream about her?"

Stoddard spit and rinsed his mouth. He put his toothbrush away, then turned to face her. "Jealous?"

"No."

"C'mon," Stoddard said. "You can tell me if you are. It's just us."

"Fuck you," Corbin said, turning to go.

Stoddard reached her before she could clear the door and caught her wrist. She whirled and slapped at him with her free hand. He caught her hand easily, like stopping a child. She was five feet seven, 115 pounds, and looked—*felt*—incredibly small up against him.

"Listen," Stoddard growled.

"Fuck you."

Stoddard slapped her, just hard enough to get her attention. Redness appeared on her cheek.

"Don't you do that again," she warned in a cold voice. Maybe she wasn't a martial-arts queen, but Jacy Corbin was the kind of a woman who could get next to a man then shove a stiletto through his neck and slice his windpipe in two. Going to sleep next to her, knowing that, was something of a rush.

"Don't you accuse me of being less than professional," Stoddard said. "Don't play little games like this, Jacy. The Zhao woman is just a job. Just like her brother was before her. I lost her brother, remember? We lost her brother. Maybe I worry about that. I'm section chief over this op, and this little political excursion isn't paying off too well. Maybe that's weighing a little heavy right now."

She glared up at him, and for a moment he could have sworn she was going to go right for his throat.

But she didn't. In the next heartbeat she melted into his arms, tiptoeing up and pressing her mouth hungrily against his. Her breasts pushed at his chest, nipples already hard.

"Wait," Stoddard said. "I've got to get my pistol."

Corbin grinned, reached out and took him in her hand. "Looks like you're pretty well armed to me." But she stepped away, moving toward the shower. "Hurry."

Stoddard returned to the bed, reached under and took out the SIG-Sauer P226 chambered in .40 S&W, then the Thermos-size satellite phone that kept him in touch with the operation in Hong Kong. By the time he returned to the bathroom, Corbin already had the shower going.

"A shower," she said as he stepped into the steam-fogged shower cubicle, "then breakfast somewhere on Hong Kong Island. Post 97. You like it there. My treat."

"Sure," Stoddard said. He put the SIG-Sauer and the sat-phone on the ledge above the hot spray of the showerhead. The needle spray plowed into him, relaxing him almost instantly.

Corbin cupped him in her hand, knelt, then took him into her mouth. He felt himself reacting almost at once and gave himself over to the hunger that scratched through him with cat's claws.

She wasn't the first fellow agent Stoddard had taken on as a lover during his sixteen-year career, and he never even entertained the idea that she would be the last. He didn't have relationships. He only found things to do, people to do, while waiting for the action to heat up again. And right now doing Jacy was plenty. She kept him running at peak condition, kept the sexual edge off enough that he could relax during the present mission when everything had turned into such a cluster-fuck.

Losing Syn-Tek Zhao, Saengkeo's brother and head of the Moon Shadow Triad, hadn't been in the plans, but that unhappy occurrence had sure as hell shown up in the cards. Syn-Tek had been a good listener, and he'd seen the logic in what Stoddard was doing until the very end.

But Saengkeo Zhao? That woman was hardheaded. She didn't trust anybody outside of her own skin. The only reason she was working with him was because of what he had to offer. Or rather, what the United States had to offer through Stoddard. For now, he had her attention, but he didn't have her compliance, and that was eating him up.

He shifted gears mentally, trying to pay attention to what Jacy was offering. They'd been lovers for eight months, most of them spent in Hong Kong working the angles to set up the present operations, stretching thin occasionally all the way up to Russia. She was good in Russia, spoke the language like a native and fit in with them easily with her pale skin, blond hair, and whatever color eyes she chose to wear that day.

Without warning, leaving Stoddard hovering on the brink, Corbin stood. She smiled at him, water beading over her breasts from the hot spray and bleeding down her cleavage.

"You're too ready this morning," she said coyly. "And I know from experience that you can be selfish." Then she hooked an arm behind his neck, wrapped a leg around his waist, and pulled herself up him. He leaned back only a little as she joined them. Holding to him tightly, she started a rhythmic up and down motion that plunged him deeply within her then drew her off. Her quivering muscles and panting breath let him know she was close, too.

The sat-phone rang, sounding harsh and strident in the bathroom against the hiss of the shower.

Automatically, switching off everything else, mind taking over and putting his body on auto-pilot even though Jacy didn't stop rising and falling, Stoddard pulled the phone to his ear. The team had a good communications relay in place and the encrypted sat-phone never rang—unless there was a problem.

"Stoddard," he said into the mouthpiece, water running down his chin, slapping inside his mouth.

"We've got a problem," Dave Kelso said. He was a ten-year veteran in the Asian theater, part Chinese himself but every bit of it by way of American culture.

"What?"

"The Zhao woman just got a phone call from Yang," Kelso said. "He wants a meet."

"They're already meeting." Stoddard knew all about the Triad meeting scheduled for later that day. He'd planned to be there, to watch and to listen in, staying on top of the game he'd so carefully set up.

"Yang wants a one-to-one party."

"She won't agree to that."

"She did. Yang held up some woman named Pei-Ling Bao as bait."

"Does he know where she is?"

"Don't know, boss," Kelso answered.

Stoddard felt Jacy convulse against him, hitting her peak and shuddering through without him. He only felt minor irritation. Worst of all was Saengkeo Zhao's decision to meet with Yang. Yang hated her, wanted her as dead as her brother so he could take over her family's holdings.

If something happened to Saengkeo Zhao, Stoddard didn't believe that the Moon Shadow Triad would go down without a fight, but without Saengkeo Zhao to pull all the contingent parts together, to get them to act as one, there was a good possibility that Yang could achieve his objective.

"I'm on my way," Stoddard said.

Corbin slid off him, a mocking smile on her face.

"Keep her covered till I get there," Stoddard went on.

Kelso sighed. "We can't. A couple minutes ago, she ditched us. I don't know where she is."

Stoddard cursed. The damn woman couldn't be a team player. Everything was right there. All they had to do was stay on target. "Do you know where the meeting place is?"

"Yeah. Central. Exchange Square. Hadley's already confirmed that Yang is there."

"But Saengkeo Zhao isn't there?"

"No, sir."

Stoddard took a deep breath and ran his free hand through his hair. He reached up for the SIG-Sauer, keeping the weapon from the shower spray. He knew he'd have to clean the pistol later because of the condensation from the shower.

"Then sit on Yang," Stoddard said. "Let's take what we

have until we can find her." He punched the disconnect button, thoughts whirling, feeling as if the bottom had just dropped out of his world.

"The Zhao woman is missing?" Corbin asked, already in motion herself. She took her own pistol from a shelf in the shower, proving that she'd learned from him and that she'd intended for them to end up showering together this morning despite the argumentative mood she'd been in.

"Not missing," Stoddard said. "She took off."

"Where?"

"I don't know. But with that woman, you know it's not going to be good."

SAENGKEO ZHAO left the Mercedes parked illegally at the Aberdeen Harbour pier. A half-dozen fishermen yelled at her, telling her that she couldn't leave the vehicle there. She ignored them because any police officer who ran her license plate would discover whom the car belonged to and would be more inclined to protect the Mercedes than to have the vehicle hauled away. The markets, the fishing and the cargo handling were fully under way now. Pedestrian traffic was heavy.

Ships filled Aberdeen Harbour. The sight was a familiar one to her because she'd grown up around the docks. Tugboats, sampans and junks littered the harbor, staying away from the cargo ships that plied the water. Some of the larger freighters sat farther out, attended to by crews working from lighters, the small cargo transfer ships. Most of the cargo ships unloaded on the other side of the island at Central, but many businesses refused to pay or provide trucking that would bring it across the island.

Fishermen lived half their lives in and around their boats. Sailors lived considerably longer aboard their vessels when they were signed to a crew. But some of the families had lived in the harbor for generations, stepping onto dry land only to take on supplies or trade for things they needed.

The family-owned boats moved only a little, enough to fish and trade and get supplies. For the most part, the vessels were squat, ugly boats made from whatever had come to hand, then repaired and reworked with the same. Small children ran around the decks wearing rope leashes that tied them to the boats. The leashes weren't inhumane; they were safety cords. That way if they fell into the harbor they, or someone else aboard, had a chance to pull themselves back up before drowning.

During her days in the harbor with Ea-Han, Saengkeo had seen two drowned children. The experience had been horrible and caused her nightmares for weeks each time. The people who lived on their boats now, she realized, weren't much different from the boat people of Chi-Kan Zhao's time. All of those people, past and present, had been driven from the land by the wealthy and stronger. Skyscrapers had risen in the city and sails had been given up for small engines, but their lives had changed hardly at all.

The fact was sad, and served to remind Saengkeo why she and her brother and her father had worked so hard to do the things they had with the family's interests. And now Wai-Lim Yang thought he could step into her world and start forcibly bargaining with her.

She turned her thoughts from the past and from sadness, concentrating on what she had to do.

Johnny Kwan waited in a sleek powerboat at the end of the pier. He was tall and compact, with a generous, easygoing smile. The thick salt air pulled at the black windbreaker he wore over black martial-arts pajamas and tossed his black hair around.

"Have you found *Goldfish?*" Saengkeo asked as she crossed the bobbing boardwalk, then stepped down into the powerboat.

"Yes," Kwan said. Although known as a jokester, he was all business at the moment.

When Syn-Tek had been alive, Kwan had been her brother's right-hand man when matters of physical danger arose. Only Syn-Tek's orders that Kwan stay with Saengkeo the night her brother was murdered had kept Kwan alive. Otherwise, Saengkeo felt certain, Kwan would have met the same fate as her brother and the men he'd taken with him. Still, the loss of face at not dying with his friend and benefactor was hard for Kwan to take.

"Thank you for coming so quickly," Saengkeo said.

"Any time you need me," Kwan said. "I promised that."

Normally, before Syn-Tek's death, he might have told her a joke. This day, as many days before, there were no jokes. Saengkeo missed the jokes, and she missed Kwan's smile.

Kwan called up orders to the helmsman, and the luxury boat powered out of the harbor, slipping effortlessly by fishing boats, junks and cargo ships.

Gazing at the crew, Saengkeo's trained eye took in the fact that they were all heavily armed. Of course, for the course of action that she had called in to Kwan, they'd have to be.

"Where is *Goldfish*?" Saengkeo asked, crossing the pitching deck to the door that led down into the small cabin.

"On this side of the island," Kwan answered.

Goldfish was one of Yang's prize pleasure ships. The vessel maintained a staff of prostitutes that serviced ships' captains and high rollers on vacation. A small group of croupiers and dealers on board provided some gambling, but the ship primarily turned a profit from the flesh trade conducted in the small but elegant rooms.

Although each of the Hong Kong triads had a finger in every criminal pie throughout the city, each triad also had a tendency to specialize. Yang's specialty was prostitution, followed closely by gambling and loan-sharking. The specialty of the Moon Shadow triad tended to be transportation of illegal goods, but it hadn't remained free of many crimes over the years and had gotten heavily involved in the opium trade in the middle of the nineteenth century. But that had ended in the 1920s when her great-grandfather had moved their family from Shanghai to Hong Kong and stepped away from the opium business.

"You brought clothes for me?" Saengkeo asked.

"Belowdecks. They are laid out for you."

"Set the course for *Goldfish* and get us under way."

Kwan nodded but hesitated. "Are you sure this is the course of action to follow?"

Saengkeo looked at the man. Her brother had known Kwan better than she did. "Perhaps my brother would not have pursued such a move," she said quietly so that none of the other men aboard the boat could hear, "but he lived in different times."

A question flickered through Kwan's eyes but he didn't say anything.

"Those times," Saengkeo explained, "were the times when my brother was alive, and we knew who all of our enemies were."

Slowly Kwan nodded in agreement.

"Someone murdered Syn-Tek," Saengkeo said. "They took him from us. Someone he trusted."

"He would not have trusted Yang," Kwan said.

"But Yang could have hired someone my brother trusted."

"I want to argue with that. No one Syn-Tek trusted would have betrayed him."

"Go ahead and argue," Saengkeo invited. "Syn-Tek will be no less dead and we'll be no closer to an explanation of why he was taken from us or by whom. An enemy could not have gotten close enough to my brother to kill him as he was killed. He would not have let a stranger close to him. And he would have killed an enemy at that range." She remembered the powder burns around the tears in Syn-Tek's clothing that testified to the proximity of his killer. "And Yang says he knows where Pei-Ling Bao is."

A frown flickered across Kwan's face for just a moment, then disappeared. He'd never cared for Pei-Ling.

"Yang wanted to blackmail me," Saengkeo said, "to trade me the information of where Pei-Ling is for my support in the meeting later today."

"You could have told him no."

"I'm going to." Turning, Saengkeo went belowdecks to the small but spacious cabin trimmed in red lacquer wood. The boat had belonged to her brother, a gift from their father.

Stripping quickly, Saengkeo took up the black tight-legged paratrooper's pants and a pullover black sweater that hugged her curves. She stepped into a pair of lightweight hiking boots, then laced them up tightly. She pulled on a Kevlar vest, then added the double shoulder rig for the Walther Model P-990 QPQs. After shrugging into a black windbreaker to cover all her gear, she returned to the top deck.

Kwan stood on the port side of the boat and talked into a compact, heavy-duty walkie-talkie.

Gazing around, away from the hustle and bustle of the harbor area, Saengkeo clearly saw the three other boats closing in on *Goldfish*. All of them held a contingent of Moon Shadow warriors on board.

Goldfish cruised slowly, moving along the outer edge of Aberdeen Harbour. Lighters waited in readiness at the docks, awaiting a radio call to ferry passengers in or out as berths opened up or passengers finished their business aboard the ship.

Goldfish was a twin-hulled small passenger ship, what some people termed the mini-cruise ship. Yang had always loved boats and ships, and as a result had a tendency to sink extra profits in a flotilla of craft. *Goldfish* was the crown jewel in his fleet. The boat had been built only six years earlier and had a passenger and crew capacity of one hundred. Most of the passengers and entertainers were inside the ship, leaving only a handful of men to crew the ship.

"They've seen us," Kwan stated softly.

Saengkeo remained silent. With the open water around them, there had been no chance at all of them taking the ship completely unawares.

"We're taking the boat," she said. "Yang is going to learn the cost of his attempted blackmail." She paused, watching as their pilot throttled down the powerboat's engines to match the fifteen or so knots the mini-cruise ship maintained.

All of the ship's crew wore dress whites, making them look resplendent and totally legitimate. Two of the men lifted binoculars and studied the four ships closing in on them. The ship's decks held men and women in lounge chairs. The women wore bikinis and a number of them went topless. With the kind of bribe money Yang paid, the harbor patrol wouldn't say anything. Other women, scantily dressed, served drinks. Saengkeo knew there would be others belowdecks in the gambling areas and the private rooms.

Kwan listened to his walkie-talkie for a moment, then turned to Saengkeo. "*Goldfish* is hailing us on all channels," he said.

"Ignore them," Saengkeo said. "They'll know what we're doing soon enough." She took a deep breath. "Okay. Give the order. Close in. I don't want any shooting if we can help it, but if shooting becomes necessary, tell the men to shoot to kill. I don't want any tourists harmed."

Speaking rapidly, Kwan relayed the orders. When he finished, he reached into the duffel bag at his feet, took out two short swords and passed one to Saengkeo. He knew she could use blades because they'd studied together for a time.

Saengkeo pulled the straps of the sword case over her shoulders, giving herself room to draw the weapon easily. The sword would be a last defense, but the weapon's presence could also be immediately disheartening and threatening. Then the powerboat's diesel engines roared, powering the hull across the water as they closed on the mini-cruise ship.

Johnny Kwan waved a hand.

Instantly gunfire aboard the powerboat rattled across the sea as the men Kwan had stationed inside the pilot's bridge unlimbered their weapons and fired.

Crimson blossomed on the breasts of the men's crisp white uniforms as bullets ripped through them. Even with the advent of sudden death, some of Yang's security people managed to get off a blistering salvo that chipped and chewed into the powerboat.

Saengkeo took cover behind the powerboat's pilothouse, pushing her breath out and drawing in air deeply to recharge her lungs. This far out into the harbor, few people would take notice of the noise or even recognize the gunshots. Those who did notice would concern themselves with their own problems. And Yang paid the harbor patrol to stay away from his business.

Kwan barked orders through the walkie-talkie, urging the gunners to fire again.

The second volley of gunfire cleared the mini-cruise ship's decks of armed security people for a moment. The guests scrambled from their lounge chairs, most of them wobbling drunkenly or under the influence of narcotics as they tried to take cover.

The powerboat butted up against the vessel. Saengkeo felt the shiver of impact, then boarding ladders made of nylon rope and wooden steps were thrown over the high sides.

Kwan looked at Saengkeo, awaiting her orders.

"Do it," she said, dry mouthed. Of all the violence that she'd been involved in while working first at her father's side, then at her brother's, she'd never taken part in a boarding crew of an enemy vessel.

Kwan called orders to the other men over the walkie-talkie, then rushed forward to the nearest of the three rope ladders.

Without a second thought, Saengkeo drew both her pistols and followed at Kwan's heels.

4

Saengkeo Zhao hooked her hands over the wooden slats of the rope ladder hanging from the ship. The throbbing roar of the minicruiser and the powerboat keeping pace with the bigger vessel filled her ears. If she hadn't been wearing the headset radio, she wouldn't have heard Kwan's commands to the men.

As she climbed, the triad leader glanced forward, watching as black-clad fighters scrambled up the rope ladder hanging from *Goldfish*'s prow section. Conversation over the radio uplink let her know the other two boats had reached the minicruiser and were boarding, as well.

The pitch and yaw of the two vessels and the deep water caused both craft to slam against each other. If the crew aboard *Goldfish* had been given more time, they could have probably used the ship's greater size and weight as weapons against the powerboats.

One of the Moon Shadow gunners tumbled from the rope

ladder hanging from the prow and disappeared under the water. Saengkeo hoped the man thought to dive deep before the powerboat hit him. Then she reached the top of the ladder, throwing her arm over the side and pulling herself up. *Goldfish*'s guests screamed in fear, their eyes wide in terror. The natives to Hong Kong knew that pirates operated in the South China Sea, and the visiting tourists had all heard rumors.

Saengkeo clicked into the communications band. "Nobody dies who doesn't have to," she commanded.

ONE OF THE white-uniformed crew whirled around the pilothouse with an AK-74 chattering in his arms, filling the air with 5.45 mm rounds. Coolly Saengkeo lifted the Walther in her left hand and squeezed off two rounds. Despite the rise and fall of the minicruiser chopping across the rough water with no one at the helm, both bullets cracked through the crewman's head, blowing out the back of his skull in a scarlet rush that marred the pristine white of the pilothouse.

Blinding pain suddenly struck Saengkeo's side and knocked her back and down. She felt as if she'd been struck by a blacksmith's hammer. The Kevlar vest kept the round from penetrating, but the blunt-force trauma bruised her deeply beneath the armor. She automatically tracked the trajectory of the bullet that had hit her as she rose to her knees. Two men stood at the back of the pilothouse and fired assault rifles from the bar area set up there.

Johnny Kwan turned his own AK-74 toward the two men and unleashed controlled 3-round bursts. The bullets hammered the men backward and shattered bottles on the shelves behind them, the bar mirror dropping in gleaming shards. The mounted television jumped from the brackets and crashed to the floor.

None of the noise of the destruction reached Saengkeo's

ears. All she could hear was the roar of the assault rifles and the steady buzz of Kwan's men in the earpiece.

Under Kwan's direction, the Moon Shadow fighters split up. Half of them remained on deck to mop up the surviving pockets of resistance while Kwan led the rest of his men belowdecks.

Saengkeo remained with Kwan as they entered the wide stairwell. Kwan pressed his back and shoulders against the wall and kept the AK-74 extended before him. Taking up a similar position on the stairwell wall opposite, Saengkeo pushed her pistols out in front of her. She felt the cold chill of the wall against her nape and her shoulders where the Kevlar didn't cover. They went down the stairwell rapidly, like a well-rehearsed team. A dozen other Moon Shadow gunners followed them down.

The stairwell opened up into a dining room-bar where several guests and working girls sat at tables over a late breakfast or gambled. A long bar occupied the right wall. Morning sunlight sliced through the slitted drapes covering the bubble portholes on the wall opposite the bar. Disco music crashed through the audio system, making it almost impossible to hear any of the gun battles taking place on the upper deck.

"Get down!" Kwan ordered, then repeated the command in English, French and German.

Only the two bartenders moved, both of them going for weapons beneath the bar. Kwan swept both men with bursts from the assault rifle.

A fat Caucasian sitting at one of the blackjack tables took a step forward, grabbed the beautiful blond dealer in a slinky emerald dress and drew a short black pistol from a shoulder holster. "Anybody moves," the man said with an American accent, "and this bitch—"

Saengkeo raised her fist, knowing the man's eyes were on Johnny Kwan. She aimed and squeezed the trigger without hesitation, making the decision to shoot and shooting in the space of a drawn breath.

The .40-caliber round speared through the man's open mouth and tore through his spinal cord at the base of his skull. He lost motor control and his life at once, falling away from the blonde without harming her.

The woman stared at Saengkeo in disbelief.

Kwan stepped forward and grabbed the woman's shoulder, pushing her toward the carpeted floor. "Get down," Kwan ordered in English. He swept the assault rifle across the other diners, gamblers and prostitutes. "All of you get down *now!*"

En masse, three dozen people dropped, lying fearfully on the ground.

"Are they going to rob us?" one man asked another. "I thought you said this place was protected."

Realizing that some of the men who had paid for passage aboard Yang's floating gambling brothel might fight to keep their own property, Saengkeo crossed the room to the bar and tore out the wires to the audio deck. The music died.

Saengkeo spoke up in the silence. "We're not here to rob you." She provided her own translations in English, French and German. "We only want you off this ship. Follow orders and you won't be harmed. Disobey and you die."

Kwan singled out three of his men from the group. "Get them upstairs," he commanded. "Off the ship."

The men got their prisoners on their feet and moving again.

"Kwan," a man called over the headset.

"What?" Kwan took the lead again, plunging into the hallway that led to the private rooms Saengkeo had heard were aboard *Goldfish.*

"We've taken over the communications."

"Did any of Yang's men get a message out?"

"No. We were on them too quickly."

"Good."

Satisfaction filled Saengkeo. She wanted the loss of Yang's flagship to be a surprise to the man. And she wanted to let him know personally.

When they reached the first door in the hallway, Saengkeo read the warning: Authorized Personnel Only. The message was repeated in six different languages, including Japanese.

Kwan set up on one side of the door and looked at Saengkeo. She guessed that he would have probably been happier with one of his own men backing him up, or her brother, but Kwan offered no insult by requesting that she step aside.

"I've got the left side," Kwan said.

Saengkeo readied herself, raising her pistols, and nodded. "I've got the right."

Swinging around, Kwan slammed a foot against the door. The latch held through the first two attempts, but shattered on the third. Kwan followed the door inside, dropping to his knees and bringing up the assault rifle.

Leaning around the door frame, Saengkeo pointed the pistol in her right hand at the man standing in front of the far wall. She squeezed off rounds quickly, watching the crewman's head jerk above the muzzle of the pistol he held in both hands.

The two other crewmen in the room staggered backward from the impact of the vicious figure eight Kwan fired. The dead men slammed against the wall to the left as Kwan slapped the magazine release and flipped the taped magazines over, slipping the full one home.

Gun smoke hung in the still air of the cabin, and the noise echoed in Saengkeo's ears. She stepped into the room, keeping her pistols at the ready in case the crewmen weren't as dead as they seemed.

Security equipment filled two walls inside the room from floor to ceiling. A dozen monitors, all scrolling through preset menus, showed different views of the minicruise ship. Scenes of the action taking place on the main decks and in the dining room flickered on and off, replaced by views of various cabins. Some of the cabins were empty, but most were occupied by men and women engaged in sex. Two cabins afforded views of same-sex copulation in progress.

Saengkeo didn't let any of the sights touch her. Sex aboard Yang's floating flesh palace wasn't intimate. They were orchestrated acts of control and release, excesses that came with price tags. Prostitution was a primary source of income for a number of triads, as well as independent streetwalkers. Members of Saengkeo's own family still worked in the trade under the protective umbrella provided by the Moon Shadow triad.

The cabins were obviously soundproofed because the occupants carried on without interruption.

"Getting them all out is going to take time," Kwan said.

Saengkeo nodded. "How long?"

"Twenty minutes. Perhaps thirty. We'll have to get a cargo ship in to transfer the passengers and crew."

"Twenty," Saengkeo responded. "I want them off the ship. Alive. Even if you have to pitch them overboard in life vests."

Kwan didn't argue. He turned and gave orders to his men, splitting them into teams that would back each other as they progressed down the current deck, then onto the lower one.

"I need a cell phone," Saengkeo said.

Kwan dug a phone from inside his shirt and passed over the device.

Saengkeo keyed the phone, punched in Yang's number and closed the broken door of the security room as well as she could. There was little static on the line, and the soundproofing of the room dimmed the gunfire.

A female receptionist with a British accent answered the phone in English.

"Mr. Yang," Saengkeo said, speaking in English.

"Mr. Yang is busy, I'm afraid. May I have your name?"

"Mr. Yang is sitting in Central, in Exchange Square, and he's waiting to have a meeting with me. My name is Saengkeo Zhao." Crossing to the room's only window, the triad leader stared across the water. In the distance she saw the imposing bulk of Victoria Peak ringed with clouds of fog and smog from the city below. No ships approached the mini-cruiser, and Kwan's lookouts confirmed that no one had taken undue interest in the vessels. Transport ships often ferried Yang's paying guests back and forth to the island and the mainland.

The receptionist excused herself and put Saengkeo on hold. A moment later, the connection was resumed.

"Mr. Yang will speak to you," the receptionist said. "I apologize for any inconvenience I might have caused this morning. I will transfer you to Mr. Yang's phone immediately."

Saengkeo waited through the clicks, then heard the buzz of the transferred connection.

"Saengkeo," Yang said irritably, "where are you? I've been waiting for almost fifteen minutes."

"I'm sorry," Saengkeo said. She only apologized so that Yang would believe he had the upper hand for a moment. He would probably think she was busy checking with her sources concerning Pei-Ling's whereabouts before she made herself in any way beholden to him. That was what he would have done. "Something came up."

"Are you going to be here?" Yang sounded as petulant as a child. Now that he thought he had the upper hand, he was impatient to exercise his authority.

"Yes." Saengkeo watched the security monitors as Kwan and his team went room to room and evicted the people. One man tried to take a stand against Kwan only to have Kwan buttstroke him with the assault rifle and drop him in an unconscious heap. "I'll only be a short while longer."

"How much longer? Time is money, and I set aside my morning to have this meeting with you when I should be preparing for the meeting this afternoon."

"Thirty minutes," Saengkeo said.

"Thirty minutes is too long," Yang complained.

Since he had said nothing of *Goldfish*, Saengkeo knew he hadn't heard about the minicruise ship being taken. "That's the best I can do," she said. "Perhaps this meeting should be postponed to another time."

"Don't you wish to know what happened to your friend?"

"Yes." Saengkeo let the answer hang. Yang knew how much she wanted the information. Otherwise he would never have come to her.

Yang sighed, letting her hear the full brunt of his displeasure. "This is a major inconvenience, but I will wait. Thirty minutes. One tick of the clock after that and I am gone."

"That will be fine," Saengkeo said, and she broke the connection.

New York

THE RUSSIAN ROSE to his feet in the cell as Bolan entered the room. As small as the room was, the big warrior seemed larger than ever. Despite the weak light in the room, Bolan kept on his sunglasses. He didn't speak, just stood at rest with his hands clasped in front of him. In the Executioner's experience, silence was often more threatening than anything he might offer. The creative force of a man who had killed people, some of them as horribly as Pribik Askenov, had been at work on the Russian's mind since he'd been placed in the cell.

Behind Bolan, Leo Turrin closed the door. The snick of the lock sliding home sounded loud in the emptiness of the cell.

Leaning back against the wall, Askenov tried to be tough. He crossed his arms and shrugged. "You have not killed me yet."

"No," Bolan agreed. "But you haven't earned a free pass out of here yet, either."

"You can't make me talk." Askenov cut his eyes from Bolan to Turrin and back again.

"No," Bolan said. "And we have no guarantees that you haven't lied to us when you do talk."

"And if I decide not to talk?"

"You die." Bolan stripped the answer of any emotion, making the reply hard and coldly impersonal.

"What if I talk? Do I get to go free?"

"I don't have any business with you," Bolan said. "You're a means to an end."

Askenov grinned, but the effort was weak, showing the nervous fear underneath like peeling paint. "Yet, here I am, with no way of knowing if you're lying to me."

"Only one way to find out," Bolan suggested.

"Trust," Askenov said, "is like being a little pregnant. You either are or you aren't."

"To stay with your analogy," Turrin gritted, "I'd say in the situation that you're in now, you're pretty seriously fucked." The little Fed lounged against the wall, sinking totally into the Mafia image now and looking like nine miles of bad road. "Nobody's looking for any serious long-term relationship here. We just need the information we're after."

"And what information would that be?"

"Seven weeks ago," Bolan said, "a Russian oil freighter called *Jadviga* lost a cargo."

Askenov remained silent.

Without a word, Bolan turned to go.

"Hey," the Russian protested. "What are you doing?"

Bolan fixed the man with his gaze. "If that name means nothing to you, then we have nothing to talk about."

Hesitation showed on Askenov's face. He held his hands out, pushing the air in resignation. "Okay. Okay. Maybe I have heard of such a ship. It was attacked by pirates, was it not?"

Bolan waited, one hand still resting on the door. He knew Askenov's mind was working against the Russian now. As long as Bolan remained in the room, Askenov could believe there was a chance he would live. But after the Executioner left, the Russian would be abandoned to his own fears.

"Yes," Askenov said. "*Jadviga* was attacked by pirates."

"Who were the pirates?"

"I don't know."

"Then why were you here to negotiate with the Green Ghosts regarding the nuclear warheads that had been on board the freighter?"

"You're not with the Mafia, are you?" the Russian asked suspiciously.

Bolan gave the man the silent treatment again.

Askenov glanced at Turrin. "But you—you're with the Mafia."

Turrin remained quiet, as well, taking his lead from Bolan.

"I saved your life back in Chinatown," Bolan said.

"You saved the lives of those Italian bastards," Askenov said. "That's what you did. If you hadn't killed the Ghosts, they would have killed the Italians."

"Maybe," Bolan said. "The point being, you're in the hands of some unfriendly people. If you don't talk, I'm going to leave you here with them. They can take up where they left off. Without interference."

The Russian hooked a finger inside his shirt collar to loosen the fit. "What about if I cooperate?"

"I'll take you out of here with me."

"And let me go? Just like that?"

"No," Bolan replied. "I put you with the New York Police Department. You've got outstanding charges for drugs and weapons violations. A bench warrant for your arrest for failure to show up in court. You have to pay for that."

"You talk like a cop."

"I'm not," Bolan said.

"A federal agent could get me a better deal. Immunity. The charges dropped."

"Not me," Bolan said. "I give you a walk on this one, but you're going to fall for the other stuff."

"Maybe I'll wait for someone else," Askenov said. "Some other offer that's more favorable."

"Suit yourself," Bolan said. "I'm not wasting any time here."

Exasperation showed on the Russian's features, breaking through the fear and paranoia that had been eating him up. "Don't you fucking walk away from me."

"The deal's on the table," Bolan said. "I can't make you play, but you're going to have to want to make the ante if you want to stay in the game."

"Fucking Americans," Askenov said. He spent a little time with his mother tongue, then looked at Bolan. "You got a cigarette?"

Bolan shook his head.

Turrin passed over a crumpled pack.

"How much do you know about *Jadviga*?" Askenov asked, catching the lighter Turrin tossed over, as well.

"Tell me like I was hearing it for the first time," Bolan said. He didn't want to give up what he knew because the Russian might find a way to talk around some of the important parts of the story, hold something back. Leaving the man in the dark gave him no alternative except to tell what he did know.

"The missiles are from the *Kursk*. When the Russian navy brought her up," Askenov said, "one of the first considerations was what to do with the nuclear missiles. According to the agreements made with the Western world, they would be scrapped and the nuclear payloads would be disarmed. Mostly, I think, this was done. Some very enterprising *mafiya* members went to Murmansk and bribed the underpaid Russian soldiers. Since the economy has been liberated, some Russian generals believe they are getting paid even less for their time and continued loyalty."

Bolan watched the smoke from Askenov's cigarette pool against the concrete ceiling, creating a gray-fog island that steadily grew. The observation room had ventilation, but the cell was enclosed.

"Three warheads were salvaged and sold," Askenov said. "They were loaded aboard—"

"Sold to whom?" Bolan asked.

Askenov squinted and took another hit off his cigarette. "I don't know. I was told I didn't need to know."

Bolan watched the Russian's face, but there was nothing that indicated he'd lied.

Seeing that Bolan wasn't going to pursue the line of questioning, Askenov said, "The warheads were loaded aboard *Jadviga* and bound for South Africa. The plan was for the buyers to pick up the purchase along the way. Instead, the pirates took down the ship in the South China Sea."

"The pirates knew the warheads were on board?" Bolan asked.

"They must have," Askenov said. "*Jadviga* only carried the warheads and oil. There are other pirates out there operating that would have taken crude oil, at least some of the oil, but these people weren't after that."

"Only the warheads," Turrin said.

Askenov nodded.

"Who were the pirates?" Bolan asked.

"A Chinese triad."

"Narrow the field," Bolan suggested.

Shaking his head, Askenov said, "I can't. I was never told."

"What about the meeting with the Green Ghosts today?"

"I was told to meet with them by my superiors."

Bolan knew who the superiors were. Askenov's pedigree among the Russian *mafiya* was clear. "Do the Green Ghosts have the warheads?"

"No," Askenov replied. "But the Green Ghosts claimed to have known something about the theft. I was meeting with them about that."

"What did the Green Ghosts know?"

The Russian hesitated. "There's a woman. A Chinese woman. She's being brought into Arizona tomorrow night by snakeheads— Do you know what a snakehead is?"

Bolan nodded. Snakeheads were Chinese smugglers who handled human cargo. In recent years with all the unrest in China, the smuggling numbers had increased. Two hundred thousand people a year were smuggled to the United States, Australia and other countries. Some of the figures Bolan had seen suggested that three million people were now living illegally in Western Europe. A lot of the women ended up forced into prostitution to pay off the debts they incurred to the snakeheads. The Chinese, because of their nineteenth-century emigration to the United States and other countries that had wanted cheap labor during the Industrial Age, had set up burgeoning communities in those countries. Those communities still helped network the arrival of the illegal immigrants.

"The woman's being brought in from where?" Turrin asked.

"China," Askenov answered.

"Big place," Bolan said.

The Russian shrugged nervously, took a final drag from his cigarette, dropped it to the floor and crushed it with his foot. "Hong Kong, maybe. The people I work with? They don't always tell me everything."

"Why is the woman being brought over here?"

"I don't know. Safekeeping, maybe. Or perhaps she's being used as a hostage. The Green Ghosts have a network in Hong Kong. All the triads do. They monitor each other all the time, waiting to see who's going to be weak at the wrong time. Then they prey on each other. Things over there have been pretty shaky since Tiananmen Square, and lately the Chinese government has created special police squads to deal with riots in large cities like Shanghai and Beijing. The Big Circle Society and United Bamboo have been talking about consolidating some of the triads. In case their deals with the government fall through."

"What is the woman's name?"

Askenov shook his head. "I don't know."

"How did the Italians find out about the meeting between you and the Green Ghosts?" Bolan asked.

"The Italians and the Chinese have been feuding over drug trade in the city." The Russian shrugged. "Even when the economy goes bad, the drug trade remains good. The Italians have been watching more closely than we had thought."

Without warning, the smoke pooled against the ceiling over the Russian's head suddenly swirled.

The Executioner's combat senses flared to life instantly. Some force had shifted the smoke in the air. His right hand darted inside his jacket, fitting smoothly around the butt of the 93-R holstered under his left armpit. He pulled the gun free, turning toward the door as the thunderous boom of an explosion slammed into the room.

5

Bolan pulled the cell door open and stared out at a vision from hell. The concussive wave that had been forced under the door and stirred the cigarette smoke inside the room had come from an incendiary device. The explosion had strewed flames all over the inside of the warehouse where the stairs led down from the floor above. De Luca maintained a furniture store above that masked the other business the Mafia did there.

Darkness filled the basement. When Bolan had first entered, only a few pools of tracked lighting had alleviated the darkness. Those exploded in flaring sparks as the old wiring and fuse boxes overloaded. The flames clinging to the walls and ceiling and spilling across the floor provided enough light to die by, though.

Chinese hardmen, dressed in night black and carrying machine pistols, rushed down into the basement. The contingent of Mafia enforcers Don De Luca had provided to secure the area held for a moment because they had nowhere else to go. Then they crumpled like paper targets under the withering fire.

The Green Ghosts had arrived in force.

Bolan raked the battlefield, weighing the options open to him. Smoke crawled across the ceiling like some mythic beast. The warrior knew the basement lacked adequate ventilation to handle the volume of smoke. Once the smoke filled the area, and he was sure that would be the case, they'd all be choked down.

Muzzle-flashes strobed the darkness, seeking targets, mowing them down when they were found. The Chinese were hell-bent on total annihilation.

"Doesn't make any sense," Turrin said, clutching an Airweight Bodyguard .38 in his fist. "There's no percentage in coming here."

Bolan removed his sunglasses and shoved them in his jacket pocket. The attack didn't make sense to him, either, and he had to wonder how the Chinese had learned of De Luca's hiding place. And no matter the fact that they were going to win the battle, the cost in men was going to be high.

The encroaching smoke burned Bolan's nose and eyes. He remembered the observation room and the ventilation shaft that had been in the ceiling.

A pair of Chinese triad gangsters rushed from the darkness.

Bolan stepped in front of Turrin and lifted the 93-R. He fired a pair of rounds, putting both of them into the base of the left gunner's throat, watching the man go down even as the second gangster opened fire. At least three rounds speared into the Executioner's chest, knocking him backward. He crashed into Turrin, taking both of them down as more bullets cut the air over their heads.

Blocking the pain that screamed through his mind, ignoring the fact that for the moment his lungs were paralyzed, the Executioner concentrated on the gangster still running at them. He centered the Beretta's tritium night sights on the gangster's head and shoulder and fired a sustained burst that spit brass into the air and emptied the magazine in a heated rush.

The hollowpoint bullets caught the Chinese gangster and folded him backward. Others began moving in.

"Sarge!" Turrin called desperately.

Bolan forced himself to his knees. Pain lanced his chest, but none of the rounds had gotten in around the Kevlar vest he still wore.

A ruby light flared through the smoke that roiled around them. In places, the smoke was thick enough to obscure the light, preventing the beam from continuing on to its target.

At that moment, Pribik Askenov rushed past them, streaking toward freedom. The Russian shouted his name, waving his arms frantically.

Turrin tracked the man with the .38 but held his fire when Bolan waved him off. The warrior was convinced Askenov had given them all he had.

Then the ruby laser sight strobed through the darkness and fixed on Askenov. A heartbeat later, the Russian jerked to a standstill and put a hand to his face. When he fell, he turned, providing Bolan a quick, hellish glimpse of his bullet-ruined features.

Whoever had handled the sniper rifle was a damn good shot. There was also no doubt in Bolan's mind that Askenov had been one of the chosen targets for the invasion.

"Sarge!" Turrin cried out, fisting Bolan's jacket and yanking him back toward the safety of the cell.

The Executioner pushed his friend's hand away and stood on his own power. His breath returned to him in a rush, but the smoke started a coughing attack.

Turrin examined Bolan.

"Vest," Bolan said. "Still had it on from earlier."

"Shit. You scared the hell out of me."

"I knew you didn't have a vest." Bolan reloaded the Beretta. "Come on." He fired into the smoke, targeting the muzzle-flashes he saw there, keeping the Chinese gangsters honest.

No one else tried to rush their position, but Bolan knew that was as much because of the smoke and the fire as anything else.

He led the way to the observation room. Another cannonade of explosions ripped through the warehouse, letting him know the Green Ghost triad hadn't come there to do anything by half measures.

Inside the observation room, Bolan closed and locked the door. If the triad gangsters chose to rush them, he knew the door wouldn't hold for long, and barely served to hold back the barrage of rounds that hammered against the thick wood. Luckily the door was ancient, made of hardwood instead of a flimsy hollow-core replacement.

Bolan holstered the Beretta, shoved the laptop and digital camera into a leather backpack and climbed onto the folding table. Not designed for such hard use, the table quivered threateningly but held. The Executioner stuck his head and shoulders into the swirling layer of smoke trapped against the ceiling.

He took a Cold Steel Tanto knife from a sheath on his right calf and a penlight from his shirt pocket. Jamming the blade under the edge of the ventilation cover and holding the penlight in his mouth, he raked the knife's edge against the screws holding the cover closed. Although the blade hadn't been intended to cut through metal, it sheared through the screws with little effort.

The ventilation cover came free, dropping into his hands. He tossed the metal grate to one side and sheathed the knife. Bullets continued to hammer the door as he took the penlight from his mouth and peered up into the ventilation shaft.

Thankfully the shaft provided enough space to crawl.

Bolan reached up and tested the edges, hoping they were solid and wouldn't just tear loose. They held even when he put all of his weight on them.

"Think the shaft leads out?" Turrin asked.

"I checked the blueprints earlier," Bolan said. After he'd learned which building was being used, getting the blueprints from Kurtzman had been simple. He'd never liked the idea of walking into a place or a situation that he didn't have a plan for walking back out of. "The shaft is an original installation. Goes through to the roof."

Turrin started on a coughing jag. When he finished, he said, "What are we waiting for?"

Bolan's sinuses and lungs burned from the smoke, but he felt hopeful about the draft going through the ventilation shaft. There still remained the possibility of being overcome by the smoke while they climbed. Turrin handed up the backpack and the Executioner pulled himself into the shaft. He paused, extending a hand and pulling Turrin up after him.

The effort and lack of oxygen made Bolan's senses swim. Under the Kevlar vest, the bruises across his chest throbbed painfully. He settled the backpack's weight over his shoulder and continued up, listening to Turrin's labored breathing behind him.

Hong Kong

"I'VE GOT HER."

Rance Stoddard looked away from Wai-Lim Yang, who was seated at one of the outdoors cafés in Exchange Square.

The part of Hong Kong he was in, called Central because of the main street that ran through the area, was the largest tourist trap on the island. At 9:10 a.m., Central was already buzzing with vacationers and businessmen meeting with clients over power brunches.

"Where is she?" Stoddard asked. His radio was mocked up to look like an MP3 player, lending him the touristy look in his khaki pants and golf shirt. The lightweight black windbreaker concealed the SIG-Sauer in a paddle holster at the small of his back.

"East," David Kelso said over the radio link. "Back toward the Star Ferry. She's wearing some kind of spotted coat."

"That's a patchwork kimono jacket," Jacy Corbin said. "Our girl has always been something of a flashy dresser."

Stoddard caught the undercurrent of sarcasm in the female agent's words. He was aware that the rest of his team had probably heard the inflection, as well, but sarcastic commentary was part of what Jacy was all about. Stoddard didn't think any of the rest of the team knew he was sleeping with her, but if they did, they kept the knowledge to themselves. Field agents left in place for long periods of time often sought out their own liaisons, either with each other or with the indigenous population. As long as their private moments didn't interrupt the case load, no one said anything.

Moving through the crowd, Stoddard closed on Saengkeo, spotting the woman now among the thronging pedestrians. She wore the jacket Kelso had described, a top that hugged her bosom and tight leather pants. If Stoddard hadn't known her age, he would have guessed she was a college student.

Pausing by an herbal tea café, Stoddard let Saengkeo pass. "Have any of Yang's men seen her yet?"

"Negative," Kelso replied. "Yang's men are staying close to their boss."

Stoddard turned and fell into step with Saengkeo. Within three strides, he was close enough to her to reach for her elbow.

Instead, Saengkeo sidestepped him, moving from her chosen direction into a tourist shop specializing in T-shirts and souvenirs.

Anger surged through Stoddard as he had no choice but to pursue her. Once inside the shop, out of sight of Yang's men if they happened to spot her, she wheeled on him, waving back the two young women minding the shop counter.

"What are you doing here?" Saengkeo demanded.

Stoddard pushed his anger into a dark corner of his mind, keeping rein on the emotion. The only way to be in control, he'd learned a long time ago, was to be in control. "You're here to see Yang," he stated matter-of-factly.

"Yes. You've got my phone tapped. You know why I'm here."

"The Pei-Ling Bao woman?" Stoddard shook his head. "She's not worth the time and effort you're putting into her."

"That's not your decision to make."

Stoddard glanced through the window, realizing then that Saengkeo had spotted him in the reflective glass outside as he'd approached her.

"You could menace the integrity of this operation," Stoddard said. "Everything your family has worked for, the thing your brother died for, could be lost if you make the wrong move now."

"I'm aware of the risks I'm taking," the woman said.

Stoddard didn't like the look of his dark reflections trapped in her sunglasses lenses. He wasn't a believer in omens, but the image served to remind him how closely they were tied in his present operations.

"Yang is a dangerous man," the CIA agent said.

"Yang is also a clever man. If you heard the conversation

between us this morning, you know he taunted me with Pei-Ling. If I had not acted interested in this meeting, he would have suspected something and may have chosen to dig more deeply into the things I'm doing." She paused. "And if you're going to insist on broadcasting your presence in a manner like this instead of arranging to meet somewhere, Yang may find out about you anyway."

Chastened, Stoddard knew what she said was true. But he wanted to get her attention again, to remind her of how valuable he was to her. "If I'm discovered, the chances you have of getting your family out of triad business will be lessened. I'm your best chance to move quickly. Your brother knew that."

The woman didn't say anything.

"Yang may have killed Syn-Tek," Stoddard said. Though he couldn't see the pain in her eyes, he saw a muscle quiver for just a moment along her jawline. She had taken her brother's death harder than he had expected.

"If I knew for certain that Yang was responsible for my brother's death," Saengkeo said, "I would have already killed him myself."

Stoddard knew she meant it.

"The only reason Yang is alive now is because I don't know for certain that he killed Syn-Tek."

"Hey, chief," Kelso called, "Yang is getting antsy."

Stoddard glanced at his watch, knowing Saengkeo was twenty-seven minutes late from the time she'd agreed on to meet Yang.

"Where were you?" he demanded.

"I'm late," Saengkeo replied. "If I miss the meeting, Yang will only be further antagonized. You're inviting attention."

"No more than you already have."

"I'm doing what needs to be done," the woman said. "Get out of my way."

"You knew I'd be here," Stoddard said. "You knew my team would be here. That's why you talked to Yang over the cell phone knowing it was bugged."

"Yes."

"Where were you until now?"

"We'll talk," she told him. "You'll see. But not now."

"Clock's ticking," Corbin whispered in Stoddard's ear over the uplink. "Yang's getting more restless."

With the open mike he wore, Stoddard knew his team was getting both ends of the conversation.

"Cut her loose," Kelso suggested. "You own her, Rance. Maybe she doesn't know that yet, but you do. Cut her loose." Kelso had been with Stoddard the longest, knew more closely how the CIA section chief thought and reacted. "Just keep us in the game and we'll sort it all out."

Stoddard released a pent-up breath, not liking at all how things in this operation were getting away from him. This was the most layered, the most dangerous course of action he'd ever undertaken. Things had started to go wrong with Syn-Tek Zhao's death, and the thing that had gotten screwed up in New York City. He wasn't sure if he could get everything back on course.

"Go," he said, breaking eye contact and stepping behind the woman toward a T-shirt rack.

Saengkeo didn't say a word as she stepped back through the door and out into Exchange Square, merging with the pedestrian traffic.

"Watch her," Stoddard warned his team. He watched the purposeful stride the woman exhibited. "She's up to something."

The knowledge that he didn't know what she was doing

bothered him immensely. He hated feeling out of control, and there were so many things he had to keep balanced.

New York

MACK BOLAN WEDGED himself inside the ventilation shaft, pressing his back against one wall and his feet against the opposite side. The smoke was so thick he couldn't see the hand in front of his face even with the penlight clenched in his teeth. Breathing hurt, and his stomach recoiled, trying to trigger a vomiting reaction as if to clear an obstruction in his throat. Tears rolled down his face.

Only sporadic gunfire echoed along the ventilation shaft. Another explosion shivered through the building.

A momentary wisp of cool, clean air slid over Bolan's face. Instinctively he tried to draw in a breath only to feel burning at the back of his throat, and tried to retch again. He squelched the retching spasm and turned his face, seeking the source of the new air. He stretched out his hand and found the washboard surface of a grille. Drawing back his hand, he slammed his palm against it twice, popping the cover from the tracks with a metallic thud.

Metal clanged against the pebble-and-tar rooftop, but the noise didn't travel far. Besides the explosions still racking the building at the bottom of the ventilation shaft, the noise of the traffic through the streets below drowned the noise made by the grille.

Bolan pushed himself up and through the ventilation opening. He sucked in a lungful of fresh air, but turned immediately back to Turrin, shoving his head back inside the shaft. He still held the penlight gripped between his teeth, and the bright white beam splashed over the smoke roiling in the shaft.

Turrin had his back braced against one side of the shaft and his feet braced against the other. The shaft was too narrow for him to make an L, but his feet weren't much farther below.

"Leo," Bolan spoke around the penlight.

The stocky little Fed coughed violently, sliding back down a couple inches.

"Leo," Bolan called again. Every survival instinct in him screamed to get away from the smoke, that death lay in that direction. But the warrior never left men behind. A true soldier didn't.

A gout of flame wheezed into the observation room below Turrin. The ventilation shaft had gone straight up through the building, joining other smaller shafts from the rest of the furniture store.

Turrin shook his head again, coughing more. "C-can't, Sa-sa-sarge."

"Give me your hand," Bolan ordered.

Answering his friend's command, Turrin reached up. The Executioner reached down and grabbed his wrist, feeling the little Fed's own hand wrap around his forearm. Then Turrin's feet slid free of their precarious mooring.

He fell, but he dropped only to the length of his and Bolan's arms. The warrior felt the coughing spasm rack his friend. Bolan's own need for fresh air made him light-headed. Mustering his reserves, he pulled, dragging Turrin from the ventilator shaft. Both men fell to the roof's pebbled surface and lay gasping. Bolan spit the penlight from his mouth.

On his second breath of fresh air, Bolan pushed himself up and slipped off his backpack. He plucked the penlight from the roof and opened the backpack. Spots spun in front of his vision as he removed a Nikon D1X digital camera and 80-200 mm telescopic lens from the backpack. The whole operation while posing as the Mafia Black Ace was designed to be a soft probe, an attempt to gather information about who had the missing Russian warheads now. He'd come prepared.

The sniper with the ruby laser sight posed an even bigger question.

Bolan twisted the telescopic lens onto the camera, powered up the device and trotted toward the front of the building. Smoke from the burning building below poured from the ventilator shaft. The twisting gray column stood out sharply against the black night sky between the taller buildings. Farther east, the towering giants of Manhattan stood silent and still over the streets below. The glitter of Times Square created a pocket of neon lights.

"Sarge," Turrin called, crawling to his feet and hacking with the effort.

"I want the sniper," Bolan said.

Still coughing, Turrin stumbled toward the back of the building.

Bolan scanned the street two stories below in front of De Luca's furniture store. Traffic had halted. Several people left their cars or ran along the sidewalks from the apartment buildings on the other side of the street. An NYPD police cruiser, the light bar flashing red and white across the hood, turned the corner and came down the street.

"Get outta the street!" a woman yelled over the police cruiser's PA system. "Get outta the street! The fire department's gonna need in here!"

A wave of people pulled back with practiced motion. The police cruiser's siren died, but the lights continued to flash.

No one came from the front of the furniture shop below Bolan. The people inside had either gotten away or the Green Ghosts hadn't left behind anyone living.

"Not here," Bolan said. The effort of talking made his lungs revolt and triggered another coughing bout. He ran to his left. The furniture store had been framed on both sides by small alleys.

"Not here, either," Turrin reported. He abandoned his position and headed for the rooftop side opposite Bolan.

The alley below the soldier was cloaked in shadows. Small rivers of smoke poured out windows below. As the Executioner scanned the ground, another window suddenly exploded open.

Men rushed through the broken window, moving so fast they brought debris, flames and more smoke with them. Bolan watched the steady stream of bodies, then spotted the black man among them. He was long and rangy, his head shaved so smooth it glistened. He wore casual clothing, a black sweater over a shirt and dark jeans. He carried a Beretta M-21 sniper rifle over his shoulder.

Another man, this one white and heavier, burst out of the furniture store next. Bolan had no way of knowing if the guy was American, European or Russian.

Steadying himself, the Executioner focused the camera lens and shot frame after frame of the two men. The high-density camera memory card held 20 GB of memory. Shooting at 2 to 3 MB per resolution meant almost instantaneous storage of the shots and a capacity of one hundred or more frames.

Catching two running men with the heavy camera while on full magnification with a 200 mm lens was harder than finding them through a sniper scope. As when using a scope, he kept both eyes open, switching back and forth between normal vision and the magnified view with practiced ease.

The triad members leaped into three cargo vans parked farther down the alley. Rubber shrilled as the waiting drivers took off. The salt-and-pepper team ducked into a sedan. The black man tossed the M-21 sniper rifle into the sedan's back seat.

The brake lights flared as the driver changed gears, then the sedan sped from the alley, as well. The car slid broadside out in the street and nearly got sideswiped by a Volkswagen that had to run up on the curb to avoid a collision. Then the sedan was gone.

"Get them?" Turrin asked as Bolan stood.

"Maybe."

"Those guys don't belong to the Green Ghosts," Turrin said. "They don't allow anyone not Chinese."

"I know." Bolan trotted to the backpack. He scooped the bag from the ground and slung it over a shoulder, securing the digital camera and telescopic lens inside.

Shrieking sirens split the night.

Bolan led the way to the back of the building. During an earlier inspection of the premises, he'd noted the long gutter pipe that offered drainage for the rooftop. Hoping the pipe and the brackets would hold his weight, the soldier threw a leg over the roof's edge, hesitating just for a moment before he grabbed the pipe and started down hand over hand.

The Executioner's mind sifted through the possibilities. The missing nuclear warheads tied to the Russian *mafiya* and somehow to the Green Ghosts. Barbara Price's intel had over-lapped Turrin's own information to make that connection.

But why did the triad risk so much to kill Askenov? He had no guesses about that, knowing that part of the question was tied to the two men he'd spotted. And what did a mystery woman being brought into the United States by snakeheads operating out of Arizona have to do with the missing warheads?

Bolan hadn't expected much from Askenov when he'd questioned the man. But the Russian had been the only string to pull without confronting the Green Ghosts or the New York City-based *mafiya*. Now, if any of the pictures he'd taken turned out, he had two more faces to trace.

Reaching the ground, Bolan held up for just a moment as Turrin dropped the final few feet to the back alley. The stocky little Fed looked ashen in the pale moonlight that made it through the smoke streaming into the night from the burning building.

With a sudden roar, the building's rooftop came down. The falling debris created a concussive wave, smashing the fire and the heat and blowing out the windows. Bolan ducked and turned away a moment before glass shards rained down on him.

"Son of a bitch," Turrin said, gazing up at the flames reaching for the black heavens. "We were almost in the middle of that."

"They set incendiaries in the building, too," Bolan said. "They didn't intend for anyone to walk away from here."

"All over Askenov?" Turrin asked in disbelief. "He didn't know anything."

"Maybe the people who did this didn't know that," Bolan suggested. "Or maybe Askenov didn't know how much he really knew. We'll find out soon enough. Let's go. The police and fire departments are going to be all over this." Then he was moving, boots crunching against the broken glass littering the alley.

There was the wild-card play waiting out in Arizona, but with the Green Ghosts involved, the warrior had to wonder how much of the struggle had been left behind in Hong Kong. If trouble had come to New York City, something might be breaking loose there, as well. Price and Kurtzman had their fingers on the international pulse. Once they knew what they were looking for, Bolan was certain they could turn something up if whatever broke loose there was big enough.

6

Hong Kong

Saengkeo Zhao barely registered the chill sweeping in from the harbor. She concentrated on Wai-Lim Yang seated at one of the few patio tables out in the sun.

The leader of the Black Swan triad looked corpulent even in his tailored black suit, but the appearance was a deceiving one. When he wanted, Yang moved with deadly speed. A smooth sheen of gel held every hair in place, and his face was smoothly shaved. He sat relaxed, like a king deigning to see a peasant. Black sunglasses hid his eyes, but the lenses tracked Saengkeo's movements through the crowd.

Saengkeo checked the surroundings with her peripheral vision, not turning her head. As expected, Yang had eight bodyguards in the immediate area. She knew there were probably more. Yang wasn't a man to take chances.

"You are late," Yang said as she arrived at the table.

Saengkeo remained standing. "I have arrived two minutes

earlier than the thirty minutes I requested and to which you agreed."

"Making you forty-three minutes late for the original meeting time." Yang had a tendency to be inflexible when dealing with others but expected elasticity in his own commitments.

Saengkeo had never dealt directly with the Black Swan leader, but she had heard stories from Syn-Tek and her father. "Perhaps you have other business you'd rather tend."

Yang grinned up at her in amusement. "Do not try to be so hard, Saengkeo. This behavior doesn't become you."

"You want something from me," Saengkeo said.

"Ah, but actually I *have* something for you."

Saengkeo shook her head. "No. You never give something without expecting something in return. First we will negotiate that."

Yang scowled. "You are in no position to haggle."

"I think that I am."

Yang shifted in his seat and waved her comment away. "Then you're a foolish girl, Saengkeo."

Steeling herself, Saengkeo maintained control of her anger with difficulty. Too many things had been piling up: Syn-Tek's murder, the fact that her brother had been keeping her from some of the family business, Pei-Ling's unexplained disappearance and the almost crushing weight of assuming leadership and responsibility of the Moon Shadow triad.

"And what would that make you?" Saengkeo asked. "You have chosen to deal with someone you deem a fool."

The left side of Yang's face ticked in irritation. "Be very careful here, Saengkeo. Know your place."

Saengkeo said nothing. In another five minutes, Johnny Kwan would be in position with *Goldfish*. She made herself breathe out. She could last that long. The time wouldn't pass easily, but it would pass.

A young waiter dressed in a shirt that advertised the teahouse stopped by the table. He was young and amiable, and he wore American designer jeans.

"Would you like to sit, miss?" he asked in English.

Saengkeo looked at Yang, letting him know that she wasn't about to be treated so casually. There was respect in question now, and if Yang didn't recognize the fact as a man should, he would lose face.

Flustered for just a moment, knowing he needed to act, Yang pushed himself to his feet. His irritation deepened. He waved to the chair on the other side of the small glass table. "Yes," he told the waiter. "She would like to be seated."

Graciously Saengkeo allowed the waiter to seat her. Seeing Yang standing by until she was seated pleased her. The waiter took her order for strong green tea and promised to return.

On the other side of the table, Yang unbuttoned his coat again and sat. He took out a gold-plated cigarette case and a Dunhill lighter. Taking one of the cigarettes from the case, he lit up, breathing out the smoke in exaggerated pleasure. He laid the case on the table, the lighter on top.

"You see how things have gone in our country," Yang complained. "The British and American influence will never leave us." He nodded toward the Jardine House, the nearby trading house. "That building serves to remind us of them every day. And that boy." He shook his head. "Wearing American jeans like that, preferring American culture. It isn't right. Trying to be like Americans makes our young people too hard to control."

"Probably," Saengkeo suggested, "he bought those jeans from one of the black markets you operate." She glanced toward the lighter. "That Dunhill lighter is British, funneled through one of your black market sources, as well. Unless the lighter was made by one of the knockoff factories you run."

Yang scowled. "I would never carry a knockoff. Original only."

"Then you prefer a British lighter as a status symbol?"

"They make a good lighter."

"Of course," Saengkeo said with just enough sincerity that he wouldn't think she was disrespecting him.

The waiter arrived with Saengkeo's tea, precisely laying out the cup, spoon and individual teapot, milk and sugar. Before he could leave, Saengkeo paid him, tipping him generously. She refused to let Yang pay for anything.

Saengkeo added milk to her tea, stirred, offered a quiet prayer and drank.

"You have not asked about your friend," Yang said.

Saengkeo set down her cup. "You have not offered to tell me what you know."

Yang scowled again.

"You know the reason I am here," Saengkeo said. "But I don't know what you want. I know you. You will want to talk about what you want first."

"You try to be too hard to be like your father and brother, Saengkeo."

"Thank you," she said quietly. "I had not expected a compliment this early in the morning."

"I did not mean the observation to be a compliment."

Saengkeo raised an eyebrow. "Surely you didn't intend to insult me."

Yang stopped himself from an instant rebuttal. Saengkeo knew the Black Swan leader was aware that she wouldn't tolerate a direct affront. As head of the Moon Shadow triad, she couldn't allow such a thing.

"I meant the statement as one of fact, without disguised

meaning either way." Yang lied, of course, but the effort wasn't so blatant as to force recognition. "Becoming the leader of your family, guiding your triad, is a hard thing to do."

"The task I have is no harder than being the leader of the Black Swans," Saengkeo replied.

Yang struggled with his reply. In truth, the Moon Shadow organization was almost twice the size of the Black Swan triad, but Yang couldn't mention that without swallowing some of his pride. The Zhao family had built its organization to last. Some of Yang's following changed with the blowing wind.

Yang's own grandfather had split off from the Green Gang back in the 1920s when Chiang Kai-shek had taken over the Chinese government with the help of Big-Eared Du, the master of the Green Gang. The Yang family had meekly survived, pushed out of the country by the Green Gang as they consolidated their holdings.

It wasn't until the Communist Party came to power in China that the Yang family returned to Hong Kong and began again to flourish. In many ways, the old organized crime families in the city thought of the Black Swans as newcomers. That treatment among the triads irked Wai-Lim Yang to no end.

Still, with the cold ambition and ruthless tactics that Yang employed, coupled with a willingness for risk-taking and a penchant for murder, the Black Swans made easily six times as much profit as the Moon Shadows. But nearly all of Yang's profits came from illegal businesses while the Moon Shadow triad invested primarily in legitimate businesses in Hong Kong, Great Britain, Canada, the United States and Australia.

Thinking of that, Saengkeo suddenly realized what Wai-Lim Yang was there to bargain for.

"There are many similarities between our families," Yang

said. He sipped from his teacup and settled more peacefully into his seat.

Saengkeo refrained from comment, knowing that any remark she made was destined for contention. Yang wouldn't see other people's points, and he wouldn't leave until he was certain his own agenda was well-known. His attitude kept most of the other triads from willingly dealing with him. Smaller triads that had dealt with him had often found themselves bereft of the profits they'd expected, and in some instances key members of the families had ended up dead.

That thought led Saengkeo to think about her brother when she'd seen him on the morgue table only seven weeks ago. Her brother's ashen face and open, blind eyes stared into her mind's eye. The chill from the harbor swept over her with sudden strength and made her shiver. Thankfully, Yang never noticed her discomfort.

"Your family is spread out around the world," Yang stated as calmly as if he'd been talking about the weather.

Saengkeo waited, gazing out past Yang's shoulder into the harbor.

"Yet," Yang went on, "for all your assets in those American, Canadian and British cities, your family fails to take advantage of the opportunities that are available there."

"You talked to my brother about this several times," Saengkeo said. "Syn-Tek was never interested in any of the opportunities you explained to him because they carried too much risk. He explained to me everything he did in business dealings with our family."

Yang was silent for a moment.

Perhaps, Saengkeo thought, Yang hadn't known that Syn-Tek had been so forthcoming. Then her own thoughts mocked her. Her dear brother, for all the love and devotion he had shown to the family and to her, hadn't breathed a single word about the circumstances that had led to his death.

"Your brother was killed," Yang said.

"He was murdered," Saengkeo said.

"But you don't know who murdered him."

For a moment, the world was still around Saengkeo, as if she were the center of a sudden vacuum. Her lungs tightened and trapped the air inside her, not allowing her to breathe.

"You're either afraid of whoever killed your brother," Yang said, "or you don't know who it was." He leaned forward, clasping his hands on the table. The hard calluses that were mute testimony to his skill in martial arts were the yellow of old ivory along the ridges of his hands. "I want to use your assets in those cities to make money. You have established connections in those places, two small shipping lines that work between them, and I have product that I want to move. All I'm talking about is a simple business arrangement."

"And if I agree to this," Saengkeo said, barely restraining the rage that filled her, "you will tell me where Pei-Ling Bao is?"

Yang spread his hands and smiled benignly. "But of course. The knowledge of where the whore is does me no good at all. I don't care. Except for the fact that you care."

The young waiter returned to check on them. Yang waved him away with casual diffidence.

"My friend," Saengkeo stated with clear enunciation, "means a great deal to me."

"Then you do not choose your friends wisely," Yang said.

Fortunately the cell phone in Saengkeo's purse rang. Otherwise she was certain she wouldn't have been able to let the comment pass. Her brother, she knew, would have told her that such personal involvement was the result of the years she'd spent in the Western world.

"Hello," Saengkeo answered. She took a small amount of gratification when she saw the look of irritation on Yang's face.

"We are in the harbor now," Johnny Kwan said. "You should be able to see us."

Saengkeo studied the ships out in Victoria Harbour. The sun was nearly to its zenith, and the sunlight threw pools of silver over the sluggish waves. Although the harbor was filled with small craft, tugs and cargo ships, the minicruise ship stood out among them. Two other cruise ships were currently lying at anchor, awaiting the return of the tourists they'd allowed to debark, but both of those were much larger than Yang's ship.

"I do," Saengkeo said. "Everyone is clear?"

"Yes."

Even at the distance, Saengkeo saw the small powerboat sailing alongside *Goldfish.*

"We're getting clear now," Kwan said.

Out in the harbor, *Goldfish* slowed to a stop. Men scrambled from the ship and clambered into the powerboat. None of the activity drew much attention from the other ships. No Hong Kong Harbour Police boats were in view.

Saengkeo clicked the cell phone closed.

"I do not like being interrupted," Yang said petulantly.

Saengkeo leaned forward and pointed into the harbor. "Isn't that your ship?"

"What ship?" Yang didn't take his eyes from her.

"Goldfish," Saengkeo answered.

"No," Yang said, shaking his head and turning to look. *"Goldfish* is on the south side of the island today." Then he stiffened, recognizing the ship. He reached inside his jacket and brought out a cell phone. Before he could begin punching the number in, the minicruiser exploded in a mass of orange flames and black smoke.

New York

THE SOFT GLOW of the notebook computer filled the Lexus as Bolan drove through the Chelsea area of Manhattan. He was rolling north on Eighth Avenue, heading for the Lincoln Tunnel, taking the roundabout way to the airport in Newark, New Jersey. Exterior lights created a glowing nimbus above Madison Square Garden on the right.

Leo Turrin sat in the passenger seat and worked the notebook computer. The stocky little Fed dialed up the Internet through his cell phone, then launched the photo suite program that downloaded the digital camera. Postage-stamp-size pictures filled the screen quickly.

"What do the shots look like?" Bolan asked. He watched the traffic, intending to take West Thirty-fourth Street over to Tenth Avenue to the Lincoln Tunnel.

Turrin tapped a couple of keys, maximizing the pictures. "Some of them look like they turned out okay. Barb and Aaron should be able to make an ID on these guys. If they're on somebody's boards."

"Good." Bolan scooped up his own cell phone and punched in the current number he had for Stony Man Farm. The smell of smoke and reagents coming from the incendiaries the Green Ghosts had used clung to his clothing and filled the Lexus. He kept the window down slightly, letting in the cold air and running the heater in an effort to keep warm.

The phone connection rang at the other end. After three rings, the phone was picked up but no one spoke. If the silence continued or if the voice-recognition software didn't authorize contact, the call would be shunted elsewhere to one of the dozens of blinds that Aaron Kurtzman and his cybernetics team kept operational at all times. Even those blinds were rotated on a frequent and random basis.

"Striker," Bolan said.

His code name was repeated again, echoing distantly. Then there was a squeal of connection and one brief ring.

"Go ahead," Barbara Price answered. She was Stony Man Farm's mission controller. Blond and beautiful, she looked more like a runway model than an intelligence operative for the most secret organization sponsored by the White House with money earmarked from black ops.

Stony Man Farm was secreted in the Blue Ridge Mountains and took its name from the most prominent promontory in the area. On the surface and to even the most diligent observer, Stony Man Farm looked like a working farm complete with orchards and fields. A rotating group of mostly military personnel known as blacksuits, few of them knowing for sure what they actually guarded, operated the tractors and other farm equipment. They were ready to defend the Farm with their lives.

"Surprised to find you're still up," Bolan said. He didn't bother to introduce himself. The protective voice-recognition system guaranteed that she knew who was on the other end of the line.

"They say there's no rest for the wicked," Price said. "I've got a few other irons in the fire with the home teams."

The home teams were Phoenix Force and Able Team, and they worked directly out of Stony Man Farm on sanctioned missions. When necessary, Bolan joined forces with them.

"It's good to hear your voice," Bolan said.

"It's been a while since you've dropped by," she agreed.

When chance permitted, Bolan and Price were lovers, but both of them knew that relationship couldn't be anything more than what it was at the moment.

"I've got a package," Bolan said.

"What kind of package?"

"Family album. Thought maybe you could identify a few of the relatives for me."

"Let me get you an address."

Bolan waited until Price gave him an address for an FTP site. The file transfer protocol guaranteed rapid message uploads and downloads, and relative security. The encryption programming loaded into the notebook computer guaranteed the transferred data even less chance of being intercepted or translated. He read off the FTP site address to Turrin.

Turrin keyed it in, then began sending the data.

Bolan scanned the mirrors as he closed on West Thirty-fourth Street. Although there was a line of traffic behind him, his combat senses had picked something up. He kept watch, then spotted a black Dodge Caravan coming up on the right six cars back.

"Do you have any idea which branch of the family tree I should start looking in?" Price asked.

"The professionals," Bolan replied, pulling into the turn lane. "The guys we met tonight weren't local talent."

"I didn't know you had another meet scheduled for tonight."

"The Q&A turned ugly."

"Was anyone hurt?"

"We're intact," Bolan replied, watching the Dodge Caravan pull up another car length and glide effortlessly into the turn lane behind them.

"Transmitting," Turrin said.

Bolan glanced at the notebook computer screen. The horizontal task bar chugged quickly through the cycle, filling as the bytes were transmitted onto the FTP Web site.

"There won't be any more Q&A sessions, though," Bolan continued.

"Why?"

"The interview was canceled."

"Who did it?"

"I'm hoping we can find the answers in the album."

The light turned green and Bolan rolled forward, following the line of traffic. As soon as he was on the other side of the intersection, the Executioner spotted a gap in the right-hand lane. He put his foot down on the accelerator and felt the sports car's fuel injection kick in, pressing him back into the soft leather seat.

Turrin glanced at him.

"Tail," Bolan explained. "I decided to up the ante."

Turrin switched his gaze to the rearview mirror. "Got him. How long has he been there?"

"I don't know," Bolan said. In the rearview mirror, the black Dodge Caravan broke ranks with the other cars.

"It's not very likely that whoever that guy is just decided to pick somebody out of the crowd and start following them," Turrin offered.

"Not very," Bolan agreed.

"And you're too combat savvy to have missed a regular tail," Turrin went on. He glanced forward and checked the street ahead. "If you hadn't caught the tail until now, I'm guessing they didn't mean for you to until now."

Bolan nodded.

"That also means the guy back there in the Dodge Caravan isn't alone," Turrin said. "They've been gridding us, picking us up and passing us off to the next team."

"Yeah," the Executioner said.

"So how many teams do you think they have?"

"They couldn't do that kind of a job with less than three cars," Bolan said.

"Striker," Price called.

Bolan turned his attention back to the phone. "I'll call you later. See if you can match up the names on the pictures."

"I will," Price promised. "Take care."

Bolan closed the cell phone and put the instrument in the storage space between the seats. He reached up under his jacket and took out the Beretta 93-R. Despite the traffic congestion, he'd stepped up the pace, rolling past the left-hand lane.

"They had to have picked us up back at De Luca's," Turrin said.

"Yeah," Bolan agreed.

"We should have made them, Sarge," Turrin said bitterly. "Maybe we're losing a step here."

"No," Bolan said quietly. "Whoever slipped into De Luca's to kill Askenov planned to kill us. Or, at the very least, flush us into the open."

"Only when we went through the roof that screwed them up."

Bolan nodded. "They were probably set up in a loose perimeter around De Luca's, backing the salt-and-pepper team that went inside."

"That makes the other guys at four cars," Turrin said.

"Probably. Maybe five, if the salt-and-pepper team had its own car. By the time we cleared the building and the point team had spread the information around, we were rolling and the rescue units were on-site. They waited until they could catch us away from De Luca's."

"So how do you want to handle this?" Turrin asked. "Do we rabbit? Or do we rattle the cage?"

"Let's see how the play shakes out," Bolan suggested. He pulled the wheel hard to the right, taking a side street. Thankfully, the side street was nearly deserted at that time of night. Only a few cars traveled the thoroughfare. Before he reached the midpoint of the block, Bolan saw two vehicles—both boxy vans—roll out of the cross street in the intersection ahead.

The vans pulled into the street and ran side by side. One of them pulled into the oncoming lane to block the way. Both vans put their bright lights on, blasting the Lexus for a moment. Then the driver on the left threw his vehicle into a controlled skid, followed immediately by the other driver. When both vehicles rocked to a stop, they presented a solid line that blocked the narrow street, guaranteeing that Bolan couldn't pass without crashing into one or both of them.

"Shit," Turrin said, bracing a hand against the console. "Gonna have to play this one out the hard way."

Hong Kong

IN STUNNED DISBELIEF, Rance Stoddard stared at the explosion out in Victoria Harbour. Flaming debris from the destroyed ship caught in the wind, flipping and turning among the white seagulls patrolling the waters for tidbits of trash and food tossed by the island's visitors.

Along the waterfront, tourists and locals froze, their attention riveted on the blazing ship. Several people started retreating from the shoreline, quickly forming a mob that swept back into the imaginary safety of the shops and buildings.

Women screamed in terror in a half-dozen languages, calling out to children who ran aimlessly. Men tried to get their wives and children to safety. Shopkeepers struggled to close their doors against the sudden influx of people, afraid of looters, as well as the potential danger of letting anyone inside who was involved with the disaster.

Stoddard knew the explosion aboard the ship was no disaster, though. At least, the explosion wasn't an act of God or a mistake. The event had been carefully orchestrated and designed. After the initial explosion, at least four other detonations had ripped through the vessel, all at strategic points designed to break the ship down to the waterline in seconds.

Flames wreathed the ship, seeming to surge up out of the water, as if some fiery deep-sea denizen had wrapped tentacles around the craft and was tugging it down. A white-plumed wake trailed the lone powerboat that sped away from the scene.

Stoddard glanced back at Saengkeo Zhao and Wai-Lim Yang seated at the teahouse table. The rest of the patrons, except for Yang's bodyguards, had fled the area. The question was why hadn't Saengkeo and Yang taken cover, as well.

Keying the mike on the MP3 player, Stoddard said, "Does anyone know what ship that was?" He'd seen Saengkeo point out into the harbor, drawing Yang's attention. And the directional mike Kelso had aimed at the table had picked up the conversation between Saengkeo and Yang. She had called the ship by name.

"Saengkeo called it *Goldfish*," Kelso said.

"It was," Corbin stated, "one of Yang's ships. *Goldfish* featured wine, women and song. With a little wagering thrown in. You're looking at what's left of one of Yang's primary moneymakers."

Stoddard stared at the burning wreckage floating out in the harbor. Black smoke still poured from the stricken ship, a half-dozen fires creating a tangled column that followed the winds and snaked toward Kowloon. Hong Kong harbor patrol boats roared from the mainland on both sides of the harbor. One of them was a large fire-fighting rig, equipped with pumps that suctioned water from the harbor to use in quenching fires.

"Saengkeo blew up the ship," Corbin said.

Stoddard couldn't believe what he was looking at. He changed his attention back to the woman seated at the table with Yang. He didn't know how he could have misjudged Saengkeo Zhao so much.

"Did you have that figured in your plans?" Corbin asked.

Stoddard didn't reply. Saengkeo Zhao was proving to be full of surprises. None of those surprises and twists were what he would have wished for. Of course, the worst seat in the house at the moment was the one Yang was in.

"Once Yang figures that the Zhao woman was responsible for destroying his ship," Kelso said, "he'll kill her."

Stoddard knew that was possible. Yang also had enough men in Exchange Square to execute Saengkeo and get away before anyone could stop them.

Saengkeo Zhao had known all of that. She had to, Stoddard decided. And yet she'd walked into the meet with Yang all alone. Not exactly alone, he amended. She had known he was going to be there with his team. Just as she had known that if Yang's men had tried to harm her, Stoddard and his team would have backed her up.

Doing that, though, would have risked exposure to the team. Even if they'd successfully eluded the Hong Kong Police Department, gotten to the mainland and escaped from the Kowloon district, they'd have been hunted. Then again, Stoddard conceded, Saengkeo was clever enough to have planned to get them exposed if she could.

She hadn't been as impressed with the amount of help Stoddard had said he could give toward protecting her people as her brother had. What had happened to Syn-Tek Zhao had been unfortunate, but Stoddard felt certain he could win the woman over, given time.

She'd played him and Yang, and she knew that he would kill Yang if the triad leader tried to have her killed. Stoddard didn't like her for the situation she'd trapped him in, but he respected her cleverness.

"Keep her covered," Stoddard ordered his crew. "Yang is liable to go ballistic."

"Yeah," Corbin said. "Yang just watched the harbor suck down millions of his dollars. Ballistic is putting the situation mildly."

Stoddard reached under his jacket and slid the SIG-Sauer free from the pistol's place at the back of his waistband. He flicked off the safety, keeping the weapon out of sight. The weapon was made even longer by the suppressor affixed to the barrel.

YANG'S FACE WAS LIVID with rage as he tore off his sunglasses. Around him, his bodyguards rose to their feet.

"Bitch!" Yang roared, pushing himself up.

Before the fat man touched her, Saengkeo slapped his hand away. She was as quick as a striking cobra, quicker than the three bodyguards who rushed forward with their pistols raised.

The sudden threat of violence drew more screams from nearby tourists.

Still moving, Saengkeo caught a handful of Yang's hair, slipped from her chair and thrust a short-barreled pistol under his chin. She turned to face the approaching guards.

Stoddard knew the guards would never see the threat in time. He tapped the transmit button on the headset and raised the SIG-Sauer. "Take them down," he ordered, and squeezed the trigger.

GET FREE BOOKS and a FREE GIFT
WHEN YOU PLAY THE...

Lucky 7

Just scratch off the silver box with a coin. Then check below to see the gifts you get!

SLOT MACHINE GAME!

YES! I have scratched off the silver box. Please send me the 2 free Gold Eagle® books and gift for which I qualify. I understand I am under no obligation to purchase any books, as explained on the back of this card.

366 ADL DRSG   **166 ADL DRSF**

FIRST NAME   LAST NAME

ADDRESS

APT.#   CITY

STATE/PROV.   ZIP/POSTAL CODE

| 7 | 7 | 7 | **Worth TWO FREE BOOKS plus a BONUS Mystery Gift!** |

Worth **TWO FREE BOOKS!**

Worth **ONE FREE BOOK!**

TRY AGAIN!

(MB-01/03)

Offer limited to one per household and not valid to current Gold Eagle® subscribers. All orders subject to approval.

© 2000 Harlequin Enterprises Ltd. ® and TM are trademarks of Gold Eagle Harlequin Enterprises Limited.

DETACH AND MAIL CARD TODAY!

The Gold Eagle Reader Service™ — Here's how it works:

Accepting your 2 free books and mystery gift places you under no obligation to buy anything. You may keep the books and gift and return the shipping statement marked "cancel." If you do not cancel, about a month later we'll send you 6 additional books and bill you just $29.94* — that's a saving of over 10% off the cover price of all 6 books! And there's no extra charge for shipping! You may cancel at any time, but if you choose to continue, every other month we'll send you 6 more books, which you may either purchase at the discount price or return to us and cancel your subscription.

*Terms and prices subject to change without notice. Sales tax applicable in N.Y. Canadian residents will be charged applicable provincial taxes and GST. Credit or debit balances in a customer's account(s) may be offset by any other outstanding balance owed by or to the customer.

If offer card is missing write to: Gold Eagle Reader Service, 3010 Walden Ave., P.O. Box 1867, Buffalo, NY 14240-1867

BUSINESS REPLY MAIL
FIRST-CLASS MAIL   PERMIT NO. 717-003   BUFFALO, NY

POSTAGE WILL BE PAID BY ADDRESSEE

GOLD EAGLE READER SERVICE
3010 WALDEN AVE
PO BOX 1867
BUFFALO NY 14240-9952

NO POSTAGE
NECESSARY
IF MAILED
IN THE
UNITED STATES

7

Saengkeo glanced past Yang, seeing the three bodyguards approaching them with pistols drawn.

"Kill her!" Yang yelled.

Saengkeo shoved the barrel of her Walther P-990 into Yang's throat. The Black Swan leader coughed and retched from the pressure. He pushed at her with his hands but lacked the leverage to get her off him. She kept him between the approaching bodyguards and herself. Seizing Yang had been a desperate move, but she had counted on Stoddard and his team being there to cover her. If she was wrong...well, she couldn't be wrong. The CIA agent had leaned on her, trying to make her understand the importance of what he'd been trying to do with Syn-Tek.

Her brother had trusted Stoddard. But the CIA agent had refused to deal with her, choosing instead to deal only with Syn-Tek. Even since her brother's death, Stoddard had kept his distance, watching her follow the course Syn-Tek had laid out for the Moon Shadow family.

Now, Saengkeo knew, lines were going to be drawn and commitments would be made. She would discover how important she was to Stoddard and his plans. Knowing that was even more important than getting her present point across to the Black Swan leader.

"Kill her!" Yang yelled again.

The bodyguards tried to flank Saengkeo. Her fingers knotted in his hair and the pistol at his throat, she made him stumble backward.

Without warning, the three bodyguards' heads snapped back and blood poured down their faces from gaping holes punched by hollowpoint rounds.

Saengkeo never heard the reports of the shots, but she watched the three men go down. She yanked Yang's hair, causing him to yelp and curse in pain.

"Tell your men to put their weapons down," Saengkeo ordered. "Tell them now, or I will kill you."

"None of your men are here," Yang protested. "If Johnny Kwan or any of the others had been here, my men would have seen them."

Saengkeo yanked on Yang's hair again, causing another groan of pain to escape his lips.

"Tell them," she ordered, shifting so that she stayed behind the man's much larger bulk.

Another bodyguard lowered his weapon, moving quickly to his right to try to get a clear shot. A bullet cored through his skull, tearing through from one temple to the other in a rush of blood that stained the stones of Exchange Square.

Yang gave the order before the dead man's body completely fell. Saengkeo felt the Black Swan leader shudder in fear.

The four remaining guards placed their weapons on the ground in front of them.

"Now have them step away from their weapons," Saengkeo ordered. "Tell them if they move toward the weapons again, they will be shot dead."

At Yang's frantic orders, the four men stepped back, keeping their hands in the air. Several people taking cover near the four men moved away hurriedly.

Sirens sounded out in Victoria Harbour, drawing Saengkeo's attention. Harbor patrol boats powered toward the burning hulk of the minicruise ship. A wide-bodied tug with a tall steel-cage tower and firefighting equipment sailed from Kowloon District. Other fishing vessels and transport craft sailed toward the vessel, as well. No one was in any danger aboard the stricken craft. Johnny Kwan and his teams had already gotten the patrons, prostitutes and crew off the ship.

"What the fuck do you think you were doing?" Yang demanded.

"Quiet," Sacngkeo ordered in a calm voice. She sounded calmer than she felt, but she held the panic away from her, trapped in the same box she had found when she'd had to identify Syn-Tek's body. The box was a place Ea-Han had taught her to have, a place that couldn't be touched by anyone or anything. Saengkeo could be whole there, removed from the world, free of conscience and free of pain.

"You'll pay for this," Yang threatened.

"Don't threaten me," Saengkeo said quietly. She pulled on his hair and thrust the pistol's muzzle more forcibly against his throat. "You will let this matter lie."

"I'm going to kill you."

"No," Saengkeo said. "You're going to realize that I let you live today when I could have taken your life. I am the master here, Yang, not you." She paused, feeling her breath tight and hot in her throat. She stared past her captive at the three remaining bodyguards, then swept the nearby area for Hong Kong police uniforms. Thankfully, there were no policemen in sight, but she knew that would change in heartbeats.

Yang was silent for a moment.

"Remember this time, Yang," Saengkeo said coldly. "Remember how my pistol barrel is dug into your throat. Remember, too, that I show no fear at your threats now. Nor will I lose sleep over them later."

"Bitch," Yang said. "You would do well to—"

Moving quickly, Saengkeo raked the pistol's gun sight against Yang's face. He yelled in pain as a bright red scratch opened from his jawline up to his ear. His body trembled, but he didn't try to get away, didn't try to grab her weapon.

"You threatened me," Saengkeo said, "and you blackmailed me over information regarding Pei-Ling Bao. My friend. I am amazed that I have suffered you to live so long."

"What you are doing is stupid," Yang said.

"Johnny Kwan told me that, too," Saengkeo said. "Johnny told me I would have to kill you. Doubtless, my father would have agreed. He didn't believe in leaving enemies behind. I'm sure you recall that."

"Yes."

"My brother never liked you."

Yang let the comment pass.

"Today," Saengkeo said, "I took your ship from you. I destroyed *Goldfish*. But I saved your money, the working girls you had aboard ship and the people who paid you to provide entertainment for them. You will get your money, and I won't take a single dollar of it. All I have cost you is a ship."

"A ship worth millions of dollars."

"Are you that foolish, Yang?" Saengkeo taunted. "Are you so foolish as to try to antagonize me into killing you?" She caught his chin on the edge of the gun sight, letting him know how easy it would be to tear his face again.

"No."

"Good. I prefer that you live, Yang. Not because I like you, but because I know where I stand with you. Syn-Tek didn't. He did not want to do business with you, but he did not want to take anything from you, either. I have no such compunctions. Not after today."

Out in the harbor, the tug equipped with the firefighting gear pulled into position beside *Goldfish*'s flaming remnants. Crew manned the water cannon and began to pump a stream of water from the harbor onto the flames. The harbor patrol boats fanned out around the craft, crews obviously searching for survivors. The PA systems blasted across the harbor, but the words were jumbled and distorted by the time they reached Exchange Square.

"If you come near me again," Saengkeo promised, "I will kill you." Yang started to say something, but she shoved her pistol into his neck and made him gag. Once he recovered, she said, "Tell me what you know about Pei-Ling Bao's disappearance."

Yang hesitated.

Saengkeo drew her pistol back and chopped Yang in the throat, careful not to hit him hard enough to break or crush his windpipe. The Black Swan leader collapsed to the ground, hacking and coughing. Saengkeo kept careful watch over the four bodyguards as she squatted beside the fat man for the cover he provided. Before Yang could recover, she pistol-whipped him across the face, scoring cuts along the man's forehead and again on the right side of his face.

"Tell me," Saengkeo ordered.

Blood dripped from Yang's face onto the stones between his hands. His body shook and trembled.

For a moment, Saengkeo thought Johnny Kwan had been

right: she would be better off killing the man and being done with him. Yang's successor wouldn't be overly motivated to avenge Yang's death because he wasn't well liked. Yang had managed to get in with several other triads and with the English and American criminal organizations, but his own people didn't care for him. He blackmailed others in his family for their support, bribed others and threatened even more.

"The whore is in the United States," Yang said. Blood bubbled from his split lips.

Saengkeo lifted the pistol.

Yang cowered from her, burying his head in his hands.

Part of Saengkeo felt bad for Yang. The man hadn't known she was capable of what she was doing. The necessity of behaving in such a manner seldom arose, and she had never done anything like this in such a public place.

"With respect, Wai-Lim Yang," Saengkeo admonished. "For my friend and for me."

After a moment's hesitation, Yang nodded.

"Where in the United States?" Saengkeo asked.

"A place called Arizona."

"What is she doing there?"

Yang hacked and spit. A spiderweb of blood appeared on the stone between his hands.

Kwan's voice whispered in the back of Saengkeo's mind. She would be better off killing the man. Yang was foolish. Perhaps he would be afraid for a time, but he would talk himself into growing braver. Or perhaps he would align himself with another triad that stood against the Moon Shadow triad. But even with her power in the community, even with the bribes that the triads paid government officials, she knew it was possible that she'd be facing grave legal threats.

If circumstances came to that, she knew she could leave the country. Leaving the country, though, wouldn't help her family. And such an action wouldn't allow her to find out who had murdered Syn-Tek.

"She was taken," Yang said.

"By whom?"

Yang shook his head and groaned in pain. "I don't know."

"Yang," she warned.

"I don't know. All I heard is that she is with a group of snakeheads taking people into the United States. The people were loaded from Hong Kong days ago, then transferred to Mexico. They went up into New Mexico from there. Tomorrow night, they're supposed to be in a place called Scottsdale."

Saengkeo knew Scottsdale. She had vacationed there. The city was filled with old and new money, and she had managed to locate some of Moon Shadow's legitimate businesses there with her father's blessings. She could call the people there and find out if what Yang told her was true.

"Why was Pei-Ling taken?" Saengkeo asked.

"I don't know. You know the whore—the girl—better than I do."

Saengkeo looked into Yang's eyes and saw the fear there. He was afraid of her. Some men, Saengkeo knew, would have enjoyed seeing such a reaction fostered in another person. She didn't.

"Find out," Saengkeo said.

"I'm not going to do you any favors." The possibility that she was weakening in her resolve seemed to encourage Yang. He straightened slowly, pushing himself to his feet. Blood wept down his face. One of her blows had cracked his wraparound sunglasses. Crimson stained his shirt collar.

"I wasn't asking you for a favor," Saengkeo corrected him. "I told you something you are going to do."

"No—"

Saengkeo released the grip she had on his hair, but she pointed the pistol squarely between his eyes. "Yes," she said, "you will. If you are able. And if you succeed, I will make it worth your time."

Yang wiped blood from his torn face. "You are not as hard as you like to believe."

Saengkeo indicated the dead bodyguards. "Perhaps you should ask them their opinion."

"You did not kill them."

"It might as well have been my finger on the trigger," Saengkeo said. And she knew that was true. Later, when she allowed her feelings to return to her, she knew she would have to deal with the guilt of her actions. But that would be later, not now.

"You go too far."

"Too far for you, Yang?" Saengkeo smiled sweetly at him.

Yang scowled at her. Some of his bluster and confidence had returned to him, but not so much that he was going to challenge her. There were still the hidden guns and men that protected her.

Deliberately Saengkeo lowered her weapon and took her purse from the table. She sheathed the pistol in her shoulder holster.

"If I find out that you are lying," Saengkeo warned, "or that you were in any way involved with Pei-Ling's abduction, you will pay."

Yang started to say something, thought better of the notion and remained quiet.

"And if I find out that you had anything at all to do with Syn-Tek's death, I will return and I will kill you. Do you understand me?"

Grudgingly, Yang nodded.

Turning, Saengkeo started to walk away. Her knees felt rubbery, but she didn't allow them to be weak. She stopped, as casually as if she'd passed a dress in a shop window that had caught her eye.

"Another thing," she said. "Never threaten me again, Yang. *Never.*" Then she continued walking from Exchange Square, directly toward the four remaining bodyguards.

At first, the four men acted as if they were going to try to stand their ground. Saengkeo thought they were trying to make a show for Yang. They knew that the guns that had taken the lives of the other men still protected her.

Yang chose not to take the chance that one of the bodyguards would wait too long to move. "Get out of her way," he ordered.

Saengkeo never broke stride as she walked through the men as they stepped aside. She kept her back straight and her knees strong despite the weakness that plagued them.

New York

LESS THAN TWENTY FEET from the two hostile vans blocking the street ahead, Bolan downshifted, grabbed the emergency brake to lock the back tires of the Lexus sports car, then floored the accelerator to tear the front wheel drive free. Rubber screamed as the tires slid across the street. Reluctantly the car's front end tore loose, gray smoke roiling from the front two tires.

The street revolved around Bolan. He glanced back at the two vans facing each other. Gunners filled the windows, looking like dark shadows on the other side of the glass. He thumbed down the driver's-side window and shoved out the Beretta 93-R. With the fire-selector switch on full-auto, he raked a blistering line of fire across the nearest van. The 9 mm hollowpoint rounds ripped through the windows easily, letting him know the vans weren't rolling with bulletproof glass.

Men jerked back from the deadly fire, and Bolan knew

most of them were hit. They'd been too confident of their victory, too certain that he would have realized he was cornered and would have given up. The hesitation also meant their first order of business hadn't been to kill him.

"Leo." Bolan tossed the empty Beretta to Turrin.

The stocky little Fed had two .38s out and ready.

"Extra magazines are in the glove box," Bolan said.

Turrin popped the glove compartment open and took out one of the extended magazines loaded inside. "We got somebody's attention," he said.

"Yeah," Bolan agreed, reaching awkwardly for the Beretta tucked under his left arm with his left hand.

"These guys aren't the Green Ghosts." Turrin shoved the magazine into the wicked little weapon, then tucked the Beretta in between Bolan's right thigh and the console.

"No." Looking forward again, Bolan spotted the headlights of the Dodge Caravan before them. With the vans blocking the end of the street, there was only one path of escape. Seeing the two cars closing behind the dark van, the Executioner knew he was almost out of time.

The attackers opened fire first. A fistful of rounds peppered the street ahead of the Lexus, followed by more that climbed up onto the vehicle's hood and chopped through the windshield.

Turrin pushed himself against the passenger-side window as Bolan pressed against the driver's side. Bullets tore through the Lexus's interior and punched through the back. The windshield became a mass of pebbled glass.

Bolan peered through the clear places on the windshield, and said, "Hold on."

"I guess we're gonna take it to them," Turrin said.

Bolan grinned. "Just retreating to the front." He stomped on the accelerator. The tires squealed as they fought for traction. Luckily the hail of bullets hadn't struck anything that impaired the engine.

When the Lexus steered straight for the van, surprise froze the driver for a moment. He started to hold the course, then yanked the wheel hard to the left, taking him away from Bolan.

The Executioner dropped the Beretta into firing position and squeezed the trigger, running through another full magazine in a heartbeat. The bullets tracked the street for a moment, then chewed into the van's front wheels, blowing them out.

Shredded rubber peeled from the van's rims. Metal bit into the street, rasping as the vehicle's weight and lack of traction pushed the van beyond the driver's control.

Bolan pulled the Beretta back into the Lexus and tossed the weapon over his shoulder into the back seat. He wrenched the wheel hard to the left and avoided locking bumpers with the van by scant inches. His move caught the other two vehicles behind the van flatfooted. Both of the men driving the cars had expected to take advantage of the van's bulk.

The one surviving front headlight on the Lexus flared across the smoke-tinted window of the sedan on the left just before muzzle-flashes exploded inside. A line of bullets drummed along the side of the luxury sports car, but they started behind Bolan's door. Before the gunners in either car could target him, he'd steered through the gap between them.

The car on the right tried to cut off Bolan but succeeded only in hitting the Lexus on the passenger-side's rear quarter panel. Metal crumpled and the car shuddered from the impact. Then the offending vehicle was behind Bolan.

"Shit," Turrin said. "If I'd have known you were planning on getting so close to the guy, I'd have shaken hands as we went by."

Bolan glanced at the chaos he'd left behind in the street.

He couldn't help feeling the strike team had been too well organized, too well informed.

Two of the attack vehicles took up the chase.

"The back seats come down," Bolan told Turrin. "There's a SAW packed in the trunk." He pulled the wheel hard, getting back out onto the cross street.

Turrin laid his seat back, unbuckled the safety harness and crawled into the back. He pulled down the back seat trunk access and brought out the hard plastic equipment trunk packed inside. Popping the latches free, he reached inside and took out the M-249 Squad Automatic Weapon.

"Still remember how to operate one of those?" Bolan asked.

"I haven't been out of the field that long," Turrin growled. He left the light machine gun's bipod locked into place and chambered the first round.

The SAW fed from a 200-round disintegrating belt directly from an ammunition box. Bolan had packed three ammo boxes. Journeying into Chinatown in Manhattan qualified as risky business, and the Executioner had been determined to spread the risk around.

"Tracers?" Turrin asked.

"Every fifth round," Bolan replied. He glanced in the rearview mirror, watching the two trailing vehicles pull closer. He hadn't completely unwound the Lexus yet, holding some of the vehicle's speed in reserve. "Hold your fire for a moment."

"Until I see the whites of their eyes?" Turrin asked.

"I'm going to make a turn up here, and I want you to have a clear field of fire."

Bullets spanged against the back of the Lexus, knocking up quick flurries of sparks. A few more rounds smashed bigger holes in the windshield. One caught the rearview mirror, tearing it from the windshield. The wind caught the mirror and dropped it into the passenger seat, along with fistfuls of squared-off safety glass.

Without warning, Bolan downshifted and cranked the wheel hard right. The Lexus's rack-and-pinion steering held the ground like a big cat, clawing around the corner. The soldier examined the nearly empty street ahead, then glanced in the side mirrors. He braked the Lexus, holding the vehicle true to provide Turrin the shooting zone he needed.

The two pursuit vehicles tried to make the corner after Bolan. Both of them skidded, turning but sliding sideways into the intersection.

"Now," Bolan said.

Turrin squeezed the trigger, unleashing a swarm of 5.56 mm hornets that tore into the two cars, ripping through the glass and sheet metal. The purple tracers burned through the air, coming so fast they almost looked like laser beams striking the two cars.

By the time the SAW blew back empty, Bolan accelerated again and reached the next intersection without any return fire. The two pursuit vehicles sat in the intersection, pooling radiator fluid and engine oil.

Turrin readied the SAW again, opening a fresh ammo box and laying the belt into the weapon's receiver. "Stick a fork in them."

Bolan nodded. "We're going to have to lose the car."

"I've got friends," Turrin replied. "Let me make a phone call and we'll have another one in a few minutes."

"No."

Turrin looked at Bolan. "Why not?"

"You heard about the *mafiya* trying to sell nukes," Bolan said, "even though that turned out not to be the case. De Luca's people heard about that and passed the information on up the ladder. Then the Green Ghosts hit De Luca's safehouse. A house that the Green Ghosts weren't even supposed to know about."

"Yeah," Turrin agreed, "but there were the other two guys we spotted."

Bolan nodded again. "But you have to ask yourself one question."

Turrin only thought for a moment. "Where did the Green Ghosts get their information about the safehouse?"

"Bingo," Bolan replied.

"So you're looking for a third party. Someone who has access to the *mafiya,* the Green Ghosts and the organization."

"I am," Bolan agreed.

"You think somebody inside De Luca's organization is feeding the Green Ghosts and these other guys intel?"

"Yeah," Bolan agreed, "I do. And until I find out that I'm wrong, we're going to stay away from Mafia connections."

"You live in a very small world, Sarge," Turrin commented.

"Maybe," Bolan agreed. "But the people I trust, I can trust all the way and never have to look back."

Turrin exhaled. "Tough way to live. At least I've got guys on both sides of the fence who can see me clear of some hurdles."

Bolan lifted the cell phone to call one of the people he most trusted in his world. Barbara Price answered on the first ring.

Hong Kong

SAENGKEO PRESSED the electronic keypad and opened the Mercedes's door. She'd parked near Exchange Square but the walk back had seemed interminable.

Out in the harbor, other fire rescue boats had joined the first. Between them, they quickly had the blaze under control. The black smoke left only faint smudges against the blue sky now.

As she reached for the door, she caught sight of Rance Stoddard's reflection in the tinted door glass. The CIA agent stepped up behind her without a sound.

"This is the second time in only minutes that you've gotten too close to me," Saengkeo said. She opened the car door and stowed her purse inside. She was careful not to get too much of her body inside the car, not to be too off balance so that he couldn't just shove her inside and crawl in after her.

Her fingertips rested on the Walther's butt. She used the jacket to cover the slight motion she made of drawing the weapon. By the time she turned to face Stoddard, she had the Walther in her jacket pocket with the safety off.

Stoddard stood in plain view before her. His hands remained in view.

Saengkeo looked past the man but saw nothing of the other people she knew he had with him. Only moments ago, those people had watched over her. Now they watched over him. She didn't doubt that those people would be just as quick to act in his defense as they had been to act in hers.

"I thought we should talk," Stoddard said.

"Not now," Saengkeo said. "We might be seen."

"By Yang?" The CIA agent seemed amused.

"Possibly," Saengkeo agreed. "Or perhaps someone else. Yang is not as secretive as he thinks he is. One of the other triads could have been watching us."

"Looking for weakness on either of your parts?"

"There are mergers going on all over the world," Saengkeo said. "The triads are no different. They are businessmen."

"Businessmen in a very bloody business," Stoddard agreed. "And most of them are carrion eaters that would feed off each other if given the opportunity."

Saengkeo shrugged. She considered dragging out some of the history she knew of the American CIA, but she chose not to. Stoddard was a man of ideology and conviction. He would be as blind in his own way to things as Yang was.

"You used me," Stoddard accused.

"Yes."

"You should have let me know what you were going to do."

"About blowing up Yang's pleasure ship?"

Stoddard nodded.

Saengkeo showed the man a thin, mirthless smile. "You wouldn't have approved."

"No." The corners of Stoddard's mouth twitched.

"And I wouldn't have let your disapproval stop me." For a moment, Saengkeo thought the man was actually going to smile.

"I'm used to your brother, Miss Zhao," Stoddard said. "There weren't many things that he kept hidden from me."

"Do you know who killed him?" Saengkeo asked.

The question took Stoddard back. "No."

"Do you know what got him killed?"

"No."

"Then I suggest to you that my brother didn't tell you everything," Saengkeo said.

"Did he tell you?" Stoddard challenged. "Everything, I mean?"

Saengkeo said nothing.

"Because if he did, then you know who killed him." Stoddard released a breath. "You and I, Miss Zhao, we share a common enemy. But I don't know who that enemy is. Perhaps if we worked together, we could find your brother's murderer."

Staring at the man, Saengkeo tried to decide if the CIA agent's words were bait to lure her into whatever web he was creating in Hong Kong, or if they were a genuine offer to join forces. Either way, she wasn't yet persuaded to take him up on his suggestion.

Her cell phone rang and she took the handset from her jacket pocket. "Yes," she said.

"You are all right?" Johnny Kwan asked.

"Yes."

"And the man with you?"

"Yes."

"He is the agent Syn-Tek was dealing with?"

"Yes." In the aftermath of Syn-Tek's murder, one of the facts that most surprised her about things was that Johnny Kwan hadn't known the CIA agent's face. Syn-Tek's dealings with the man had been very secretive. In fact, until today Saengkeo herself had only seen the man once before. But she was aware of the small effort Stoddard had made on the Moon Shadow triad's behalf. "Do you have the money?"

"Yes. I am taking pictures of him as we speak."

Saengkeo broke the connection, folded the phone and placed the device back in her pocket.

Stoddard grinned. "Was that Johnny Kwan?" He glanced around the parking area. "Is he somewhere nearby?"

"I have got to go," Saengkeo said. "I don't like discussing anything out in the open like this."

"Neither do I," Stoddard said. "But we need to have a sit-down. Soon."

"Okay," Saengkeo said. "How about dinner tonight? At the Golden Frog?"

Stoddard grinned and shook his head. "At a restaurant the Moon Shadow owns? I don't think so."

"I won't meet you on your terms," Saengkeo said.

"I know more than you do about your brother's death," Stoddard said.

The CIA agent's words cut like icy daggers through Saengkeo's flesh. She pushed her pain and suspicion away. "You said you didn't know who killed Syn-Tek."

"I don't," Stoddard replied. "But I may know why."

Saengkeo's immediate reaction was to believe that her brother's death was because of something the CIA team had been doing. "You've just seen how I've dealt with Wai-Lim Yang," she stated in a cold voice, "when he started trying to blackmail me. I won't hesitate to act in a like manner with you."

"Fair enough," Stoddard countered. "But you can't be sure that I'm not lying to you, either."

"No."

"I'm reaching into my pocket for a piece of paper," Stoddard said. He stuck only two fingers inside his shirt pocket, then withdrew them, holding a small piece of yellow paper between them. "The paper is yours but I suggest you destroy it after you've looked at it."

Saengkeo took the folded paper but made no move to look at it. The writing looked faint through the paper.

"That paper contains an address," Stoddard said. "That address contains one of the secrets your brother kept from you. Go there or send someone to check out what's there. If you decide that you want to meet with me, my phone number is listed below."

"Don't hold your breath," Saengkeo said.

Stoddard smiled and nodded. "We can arrange to meet somewhere that we both feel safe." Without another word, he turned and left. He disappeared into the crowd around Exchange Square watching the late rescue attempts out in the harbor. He never looked back. He was that certain of himself.

Saengkeo marveled at the paper in her hand. How was it that she could stand up to Yang and his hired killers, know that her course of action was going to make a vengeance-driven enemy for life, and yet one piece of paper that she hadn't even looked at frightened her?

A news van from one of the government-sponsored channels that the Chinese government had allowed to remain in place after the British left in 1997 screeched to a stop in the parking area. The reporters and cameramen scrambled from the vehicle and ran toward Exchange Square. One of the reporters ordered a cameraman to shoot footage of the activity out in the harbor.

The film would probably never be shown. The Chinese government didn't allow much in the news that showed the country or the Communist Party in a bad light. The Western nations only knew of the various riots spread throughout China from tourists, foreign news correspondents and self-styled underground revolutionaries who put up Web sites on the Internet regarding Chinese dissatisfaction with the government.

A cold wind from the harbor chased Saengkeo into the Mercedes. Yang would follow at some point with his entourage, and she didn't want to be there when they arrived. She slipped behind the wheel and buckled herself in.

Then she opened the note Stoddard had given her, not knowing what she was going to find.

But the content of the note was an address—a pier or boathouse in the Kowloon District.

Somehow that didn't seem so threatening, although she knew that the address could still bring all manner of bad things. Knowing that the note held only an address helped. But what was she going to find at the pier?

After she memorized the address, she used the lighter in the car to burn the paper in the ashtray. She drove away as the last of the paper curled up into gray-white ash. So many things still remained unknown.

8

New Jersey

"Did you get the files?"

Bolan turned down the volume slightly on the cell phone earbud he wore. Switching his attention to the notebook computer open before him on the table, he tapped the mouse touch pad and brought up the files in question.

He sat in the corner at a small restaurant in Newark International Airport. After dumping the Lexus on the other side of the Hudson River in a part of New York where the vehicle would promptly disappear, he and Turrin had taken a rental car and driven down U.S. 1 and 9 to Highway 440 and on into the airport.

Leo Turrin was at the restaurant counter waiting for the meals they'd ordered. The jet for Scottsdale that Price had arranged for was going by way of Boston, St. Louis and Oklahoma City, then made the final leg into Arizona. The flight wasn't scheduled to leave for another hour and a half. Bolan used one of the clean IDs Kurtzman had provided to get through the deep security levels guarding the airport.

Gazing at the screen, seeing the faces of the two men he'd seen running from De Luca's furniture store only a few hours ago, Bolan said, "Yes." He'd downloaded the files from the FTP site over the cell phone before calling Price to confirm the information.

Barbara Price, at the other end of the phone connection, said, "Those are two interesting individuals, Striker."

Bolan studied the two men. In the pictures, the white man wore short hair and a close-cropped goatee. The black man was smooth shaved, and was bald. The soldier skimmed the dossiers attached to both men. As usual, the intel coming out of Stony Man Farm was comprehensive and concise.

"These guys are Agency personnel?" Bolan asked, referring to the Central Intelligence Agency information that accompanied the reports. He remained deliberately oblique in case anyone was using a cell phone scanner to pick up conversations in the airport.

"Were," Price stated. "The word is that they've parted company and gone freelance."

"For whom?"

"From what I'm able to ascertain, primarily us."

"Us," the Executioner knew, didn't refer to Stony Man Farm. The reference was to black-bag operations authorized by the United States government.

Bolan tapped keys, flipping through the files he'd downloaded from the FTP site. Nearly all of the information he was looking at was top secret and wouldn't be declassified for years—if at all. In addition to the CIA service jackets and profiles on the two men, there was also some information that suggested involvement with covert ops scattered across the globe.

The white man's name was Don Marshall. The black man's name was Andre Hickerson.

"When did they go freelance?" Bolan asked.

"From what I understand," Price replied, "almost four years ago."

"Who was their Agency handler?"

"That information is buried. I turned up a few names, but I know enough about them from previous exposure to know those names aren't going to lead you anywhere. These guys have been buried."

"Why did they leave?"

"I don't have concrete information. Want my best guess?"

"I'll take it every time," Bolan replied.

"Agency politics. Looking at their jackets, you'll see these two have been cowboys. They preferred to work down and dirty."

"So maybe they got a little dirty, too?"

"That's the feel I get. When someone at the Agency went missing, these were two of the guys that were sent to bring them back—even if the people they were sent after didn't want to come back. Nobody kept these two on a short leash. I'm betting they got into trouble."

Turrin brought the trays loaded with foam containers over to the table. He sat and began passing food out, shoving over a container of pancakes, sausages and scrambled eggs.

"Where are these two people based?" Bolan asked. He took a cup of coffee from Turrin and sipped. The drink was black and scalding, an instant wake-me-up to the taste.

"I'm checking," Price replied. "Some of this information is hard to get without alerting the wrong people."

"Understood."

"But the feel is that they're domestic. As you'll see from the jackets, they're not averse to working internationally."

"Do they have a history with the players on the field tonight?"

"None that I can find."

"Someone called them in," Bolan pointed out.

"If these two men have had prior relationships to their partners and competition tonight," Price said, "we'll find that here."

"But you don't think that's the case."

"No. Not based on the data I see in their jackets. Neither of those men seem predisposed to the Company line by either their constituent base or the hard target they took down."

"That move was all about controlling information."

"What do you think your contact was withholding?"

"I think he gave me all the information he had," Bolan said. He believed Askenov had given up his greatest secret. At least, the Russian had given up part of it. "Except for where I could find the principal involved."

"I'm working on that," Price promised.

Bolan knew the Stony Man Farm mission controller was referring to her contacts within the United States Immigration and Naturalization Service. "I'll be in touch as soon as I can."

"Stay safe," Price said, then broke the connection.

Bolan pressed the End button on the cell phone, took the earbud out and put the phone away. Then he shut down and closed the notebook computer, and returned it to the backpack. Kurtzman had set the machine up to have a layered operating system. Anyone opening the computer to give the contents a cursory inspection would find only information and programming relating to business applications. Buried beneath the first layer was a heavily encrypted second layer that contained all the new files he was currently using. A trained expert could ferret out the files on the partitioned hard drive, but doing so would take days if not weeks, and by then the information would be next to useless. None of that information would ever trace back to Stony Man Farm. And failure to properly negate the top operating system would unleash a program that would destroy all information contained on the hard disk.

Turrin used a knife and a fork to cut pancakes and sausages slathered in butter and syrup. "Ex-CIA. This gets more and more interesting."

Bolan nodded and saw to his own plate, surprised at the appetite he had. Then he realized he hadn't eaten since that morning. Or maybe he'd last eaten the night before. He couldn't honestly remember.

"I can see where Langley might be interested in the whereabouts of the warheads," Turrin said, "but why call in a tag team?"

"A layer of deniability," Bolan suggested.

"Maybe," Turrin agreed. "But after September 11, seizing a wayward nuke on American soil could be counted as a coup for the intelligence agencies."

"Then those intelligence agencies would have to explain how they allowed nuclear weapons to reach American soil," Bolan pointed out.

"True." Turrin grimaced. "And if those ex-agents actually were working for Langley, that would mean we whacked the good guys."

"We didn't," Bolan said. There wasn't a doubt in his mind.

"We've always had a problem with the left hand not knowing what the right hand was doing when it comes to domestic intelligence agencies."

"This was something else," Bolan said. "Somebody trying to close down access to information."

Turrin chewed thoughtfully, then swallowed. "What information? This woman with the snakeheads in Arizona doesn't seem like the person that would know the location of the warheads. She could sell that information to someone."

"I don't think she is, either," Bolan agreed. "But she's somebody's hole card."

Turrin reached for the condiment tray on the table, pulling out packets. "We've got the Russians," the stocky little Fed said. He placed a packet of salt on the table. "And we've got the pirates that took down the Russian ship." He placed a packet of pepper on the table, butting the pepper into the salt. "And we've got the Green Ghosts operating on some kind of tangential basis." He placed an artificial sweetener a short distance from the first two packets. "And we've got this mystery ex-Agency group that's bought in." A ketchup packet joined the others on the table.

"They were brought in by someone else that you don't have on the table," Bolan said.

Turrin added a creamer. "Meaning the ex-Agency guys might not even know the score. Strictly a pay-for-play operation."

Bolan nodded. "Toss in the buyers for the weapons the Russians had for sell."

Turrin added a jelly packet.

"And you can add in De Luca," Bolan said.

Turrin gazed at the soldier. "De Luca was just trying to keep the streets safe."

"Maybe," Bolan conceded.

A deep sigh escaped Turrin. "You know, Sarge, this is getting damned complicated." He slid a sugar packet into the mix.

"One way to track the operation down," Bolan said, "would be to know who's buying the missiles."

"We don't."

"Not yet." Bolan pushed away the empty breakfast tray and surveyed the field of players as Turrin had laid them out.

"Maybe Barb and Aaron can come up with something on that front. Maybe you can here. If the buyer was here."

"That's not exactly a happy thought."

"No," Bolan agreed, "but it's one we've got to keep in mind. Until then, let's narrow the odds. The woman is important." Saying it aloud like that made him even more antsy to be on the move. Being locked in the holding pattern of the airport was almost intolerable. The only thing that made the experience a little easier to take was knowing that once he was in the air he would reach Arizona faster than if he drove.

"So who has ties to the woman?" Turrin asked.

Bolan flicked away condiment packets as he spoke.

"Not De Luca. Not the Russians, because they were going to use the information of where the woman was themselves. Not the Green Ghosts, because they were selling the information about the woman to the Russians. Not the Agency people, because if they knew about her they would have killed her."

"Maybe they already—"

"If they had," Bolan said, "they wouldn't have been here tonight to shut up Askenov."

"Okay." Turrin scratched his whisker-stubbled chin. "That line of thinking may change."

"If it does, we'll change with it." Bolan looked at the jelly and the pepper packets sitting on the table.

"That leaves us the buyers and the Chinese pirates," Turrin said.

"The buyers weren't there," Bolan replied. He flicked the jelly packet away. "And if the woman meant anything to them, she wouldn't be held. They were already committed to the deal."

"That leaves the pirates," Turrin observed.

"And the hidden party behind the ex-Agency guys who hit Askenov and made a try for us." Bolan sipped his coffee. "If the guys who terminated Askenov were closer to the woman with the snakeheads, they'd probably have taken her off the board. One way or the other." Mention of that possibility made the ticking clock working in the Executioner's head sound even louder.

"But if one of the others had the woman, they'd use her to get the merchandise back, wouldn't they?"

"Yeah."

"So you have to figure out who the woman is important to."

"She's got to be important to two people," Bolan pointed out. "She's being used against someone by someone else."

Turrin flicked the creamer, making it spin. "The people who sent the guys after Askenov?"

"Maybe," Bolan said. "Whoever sent in the guys we brushed up against might be trying to take advantage of the opportunity the woman's presence provides." He tapped the pepper packet representing the pirates. "The circumstances could be that the Chinese pirates who took down the Russians aren't as united as they should be."

Turrin raised an eyebrow. "Dishonor among thieves?"

"Wouldn't be the first time."

Leaning back in his chair, Turrin laced his fingers behind his head and smiled mirthlessly. "If there's a schism between the pirates and this woman got taken off, you can bet there's been blood spilled over it. You could start looking for the bodies to pile up."

Bolan nodded in agreement. "If I knew where to start looking. I'm going to start with the woman. If she doesn't know who betrayed her, maybe the snakeheads will."

"This is an interesting rat's nest you've stepped into, Sarge. Somebody betrayed the Russians to the Chinese pirates, too."

"The cargo that's gone missing is worth a lot of money with the political situations the way they are around the world," Bolan agreed. "There's plenty of motive."

"One thing might work in your favor."

Bolan looked at his friend. Turrin was the grandmaster of cat-and-mouse games within a paranoid organization. And since he'd played both sides—always trying to stay one step ahead of the Mafia and one step ahead of an overzealous Organized Crime Bureau officer looking to make a quick name for himself—Turrin knew all about the moves and counter-moves that went on when it came to that game.

"The thing that might work in your favor," Turrin explained, "is that not everyone who has been betrayed on this deal may know it yet. But with the way the wheels are coming off this thing, they will. All you've got to do is create a little more pressure."

"That," Bolan said, "is one of the things I do best."

Hong Kong

RANCE STODDARD LOOKED down over Hong Kong Island from the twenty-seventh-floor business office he rented in the Bank of China Tower. The office was part of the layered cover he maintained while on assignment in Asia. He also maintained offices in Macao, Singapore, Thailand and three offices in mainland China. One office was in Shanghai and two were in Beijing. The paperwork he traveled with under four different names listed him as an economic adviser.

Jacy Corbin sat at the modest executive desk against the back wall of the room. She had her feet propped up on the desk and lit a fresh cigarette from the butt of her last one.

"Those things will kill you, you know." Dave Kelso stood by the coffee machine, empty cup in hand and waiting for the pot to fill.

"These won't kill me," Corbin said. "I don't plan on living that long."

Kelso was twenty pounds overweight. He brushed his black hair straight back and could have passed for ten years younger than the actual forty-something he was. His Asian heritage showed in the epicanthic folds around his eyes and the butter-tan complexion. The suit he wore fit him perfectly, and was tailored to hide the pistol under his left armpit. With his round-lensed glasses, he could have passed as a university professor.

"You make me nervous when you talk like that," Kelso admitted. "Like you've got a death wish or something."

"Not me." Corbin blew a stream of smoke into the air. "I just look at the realities of this job. Plus, I'm kind of into the whole 'live fast, love hard, leave a good-looking corpse' mentality."

"The undertakers will appreciate your efforts, I'm sure," Kelso said.

"They say you can't take it with you," Corbin replied. "So I'm just saying maybe you should check out while you still have it."

Kelso lifted the pot and poured. He glanced up at Stoddard. "Cuppa?"

"Yeah," Stoddard growled. Most days, the bantering between Kelso and Corbin didn't bother him. This day, the exchange got on his nerves and he wished they would just shut up. Too many things depended on the outcome of the events they had set into motion. His two companions acted as if this assignment were just another walk in the park.

Kelso poured another cup and brought the coffee over on a saucer, which Stoddard accepted with a nod.

"Any sign of her?" Kelso asked.

Stoddard shook his head.

"Maybe she got scared."

"With the way she set Yang up and used us?" Corbin asked

from the desk. "Not very likely." She dropped her feet from the desk, leaned forward and grinned at Stoddard. "That is one cast-iron bitch, Kelso. Don't forget that. She's not one of the little mama-*sans* you've been playing hide-the-salami with in the singsong houses."

Kelso's proclivity for women was well-known. Stoddard was aware of the agent's tendencies and used Kelso because of them. During other missions in the past, Kelso had been able to get close to mistresses of the men and women the CIA agents had pursued. Valuable information the team had gotten on those missions had come from the pillow-talk sessions Kelso had engineered.

Stoddard noticed that Kelso looked a little uncomfortable with the female agent's rough talk. Part of the discomfort came from the fact that Kelso was almost old enough to be Corbin's father, while at the same time she had rebuffed Kelso's advances a number of times.

Stoddard knew about those advances because Corbin had told him. Of course, she'd been trying to make Stoddard jealous at the time. Or at least, tried to throw him off balance.

"Maybe she went to check on the address you gave her," Kelso suggested.

Stoddard shook his head. "There wasn't time before this meeting. I intentionally gave the address to her too late for her to do anything about it."

"Maybe Saengkeo sent someone else. Maybe she sent Johnny Kwan."

"No." Stoddard was certain of that because he had two agents watching over the address and no one had been by. He'd been in contact with the team only minutes ago by phone. No one had been near the warehouse.

"She's yanking your chain," Corbin said.

Without moving, Stoddard glanced at the woman's reflection in the window. Her image in the glass looked grayed out and almost otherworldly.

"The bitch knows you're watching," Corbin went on. "That's what part of today was all about. That's why she got us to save her ass and whack Yang's bodyguards for her. To let you know the string you've got on her works both ways."

"Saengkeo walked into the meet with Yang without Johnny Kwan," Stoddard pointed out. "She was taking an incredible risk."

"And you respect that?"

Stoddard didn't say anything.

"She knew you'd be there," Corbin said. "She knew we were listening to her phone conversation this morning."

"She didn't have a choice then."

"Just like she didn't have a choice about tipping her hand while she wired Yang's pleasure ship for total destruction?" Amusement showed on Corbin's face. "Seems like she slipped that one right by you and Yang."

Stoddard said nothing. He was aware of Kelso's image shifting in the glass. Kelso was uncomfortable with the familiarity in Corbin's disapproval with how things on the operation were being handled.

"The bitch was yanking your chain then, too," she went on. "She hung out a notice to you and Yang that she'd damn well do as she pleased, and fuck both of you." A smile spread across the woman's reflection. "I've got to say, she earned some bonus points from me for sheer moxie."

"That wasn't what happened," Stoddard said.

"The hell it wasn't." Corbin stubbed out her cigarette angrily. "That bitch walked into the confrontation with Yang, knowing she was going to blow his ship to hell and gone, and that you'd be there to cover her ass."

"She couldn't know that."

"Bullshit."

Stoddard almost lost his temper, barely managed control with great effort.

"You confirmed that for her, Stoddard," Corbin said. "When you walked up to her before she reached the meet and told her to step off, you confirmed that you would be there. That *we* would be there. She knew that the minute she walked away from you. Bet on it."

"That's enough, Agent Corbin." Stoddard made his voice harsh. He turned, a compact move that was at once smooth, efficient and threatening.

Corbin started to say something further, then closed her mouth and stood. "I'm going for some air. If something important happens, let me know." She left the room, not quite slamming the door behind her.

Kelso quietly sipped his coffee. He acted as though he hadn't heard or seen a thing.

Stoddard glanced at his watch. The meeting set for 1:00 p.m. was seven minutes away. He glanced back at the city. To the south, Victoria stood tall and fierce, overlooking the city.

"The woman is out of control," Kelso said finally.

Stoddard looked at the other agent. "I can handle Corbin."

Kelso shrugged, then caught himself. "I was talking about Saengkeo Zhao."

Releasing a pent-up breath, Stoddard relaxed a little. In all the years that they had worked together, Kelso had never seen fit to lecture him about command of a mission or of other agents. "Her brother was easier to deal with."

"For a while," Kelso agreed. "Then he got himself dead. You gave him advice, but he didn't take it. Seems to me that there's a stubborn streak that runs through the whole family."

"Saengkeo will bend. She has no choice. There's too much I have to offer her."

"Could be she doesn't see it that way."

Stoddard didn't hesitate. "She will."

"You can't afford to be too sure of yourself. There are still two nukes loose out there."

The reminder brought the stakes back to Stoddard's mind with crystal clarity. "The situation is under control. We know where those two nukes are."

"We still haven't gotten them," Kelso pointed out. "And until we do, this could still all blow up in our faces."

"We won't let that happen."

"Corbin was right about one thing," Kelso stated. "Saengkeo Zhao played us like a harp this morning. Got us to back her move against Yang all the way down the line. SynTek wouldn't have done that."

"Maybe not," Stoddard said, "but we had other problems with her brother. And his problems are what got him killed. Or maybe you don't remember that?"

"No," Kelso said evenly. "I remember that just fine."

"Good," Stoddard said. "This isn't a sloppy operation. Despite Corbin's insinuations otherwise. And if I hear you repeated her doubts and aspersions, I'll have you up on charges so fast your head will spin. Are we clear on that?"

"Crystal," Kelso replied.

"Good," Stoddard replied. "This op can make or break men. Stand by me, and when the good from this op starts rolling downhill, I'll make certain you get a watershed."

Kelso nodded.

Stoddard knew the man didn't doubt him. They'd been through too much for Kelso to think that Stoddard wouldn't do what he said he'd do as long as a breath remained in him.

"The Russians are going to try to offload their second nuke in two days," Kelso said.

"I know."

"We have to have her on board by that time," Kelso said. "Or we'll have to call for an outside team. Probably a SEAL team from one of the nuclear subs monitoring the Middle East. If we do call in a SEAL strike team, we're going to lose glory points, too."

"Saengkeo will pull in line."

Kelso rolled his wrist over and checked his watch. "I guess we'll know one way or the other in just a few minutes. If Saengkeo doesn't make this meeting, we can't count on her."

Stoddard didn't say anything. Both of them knew there was no auxiliary plan. Everything hinged on the woman. He stared out over the street, hardly seeing the traffic congestion trapped between the shops and office buildings.

Stoddard's cell phone rang. He had the device from his jacket pocket before the second ring. "Yes."

"Guess who just made the party?" Troy Jefferson drawled. He was originally from Texas, but the drawl had disappeared years ago. These days, the agent only trotted out the accent when he wanted to be annoying. He'd been with Stoddard in Asia for six years.

"Our principal?" A warm glow surged through Stoddard. When Syn-Tek had first turned up dead, the whole plan had seemed in danger. But Saengkeo Zhao had provided one alternative. Kelso wasn't entirely correct about the woman being their last chance of success for the mission, but tapping another source would upset several of the delicate balances Stoddard had established.

"Bingo," Jefferson said.

Stoddard crossed the room to the desk, pulled open a drawer and reached inside. He found the small button at the other end of the drawer. Whirs and clicks sounded behind him. By the time he turned, the wall behind the desk had opened up, revealing twenty-five security monitors in a five-by-five stack. Stoddard turned the seat around and pulled out a computer keyboard equipped with joystick controls.

During their surveillance of the Chinese triads, the CIA team had established video hookups and audio links inside the HSBC Building. They weren't the first to bug the building. In fact, some of the difficulty in setting up their own systems had been not to disturb the various other monitoring devices already in play. The setup had taken eight months to pull off, and the task was a work of art.

Stoddard keyed in passwords. The surveillance system was tied into several areas they had mapped out on Hong Kong Island, as well as the Kowloon district along the mainland. Information was a necessary ingredient of any covert op. Stoddard and his team were better at gathering intel than most other units. That was why they'd been chosen to monitor the triads.

The security monitors flickered, then burst with color as the camera feeds came on-line. All twenty-five monitors showed overlapping fields of view of the HSBC Building entrance.

Street traffic was heavy, paralleling the pedestrians filling the walkways. Stoddard surveyed the bottom row of monitors as he pulled on a single headset and pencil microphone.

"There," Kelso said, pointing to the fourth monitor.

Stoddard opened the audio links and listened to the street noises. His eyes picked up the slender form of Saengkeo Zhao stepping from the luxury limousine.

The woman stood for a moment, flanked by two massive bodyguards wearing black suits tailored to hide the weapons they carried, as well as the Kevlar body armor.

"She's nervous." Kelso stood a step behind Stoddard.

"Hell," Stoddard said, "I'm nervous, too."

"Do you think she's going to go through with it?"

"She doesn't have a choice."

"She might not see it that way."

"If she checked on the address I gave her, she knows she doesn't."

"I thought you said she hasn't."

"I said that she hasn't according to the team I've got working surveillance. Notice that you don't see Johnny Kwan anywhere around her. That's not usual."

A soft buzz filled the office briefly, coinciding with a scarlet wash that tinted the monitors for a heartbeat.

Glancing at the lower right monitor, Stoddard tapped a key. The monitor shimmered for an instant, then cleared, revealing a view outside the office door. Jacy Corbin stood at the door, gazing up at the hidden security camera. Her face was hard and defiant. She mouthed the words "Let me in."

Stoddard hesitated for just a moment. Dealing with Saengkeo Zhao, not knowing what the woman was about to do, was bad enough. Adding Jacy Corbin to the mix was just short of suicidal. And maybe realizing that was what tipped the balance. He tapped another series of keys and unlocked the office door.

Corbin walked into the room, closing the door behind her.

Stoddard closed the security locks again without looking at the female agent. Still, he felt the heat of the woman's glare against the back of his neck.

"The bitch showed," Corbin declared.

Stoddard said nothing. He crouched forward in the office chair, as tense as some predatory beast preparing to leap. He hated situations that were just out of his control. Dealing with issues that he couldn't influence was easier when they were so far out of his reach that he couldn't begin to hope to control them. But this—Saengkeo Zhao was almost his.

And the clock was ticking on the second Russian shipment.

"C'mon," Stoddard said, watching the Moon Shadow triad leader talking to her men. "What are you waiting for?"

"She knows you're watching," Corbin said smugly.

Stoddard glanced at the woman agent's reflection in the monitors before him. The situation was eerie for a moment, seeing both the women in his life that were causing him such great concern superimposed over each other. They both knew he was watching, he thought.

"She's deliberately waiting," Corbin said. "Keying you up."

Stoddard said nothing.

"That's why she hasn't checked out the address you gave her," the woman went on.

Kelso turned toward the young woman. "Why?"

Corbin folded her arms. "Because you guys keep thinking you're one step ahead of her. You're not. Maybe she doesn't know all of the ramifications of the game you've dealt her into, but she's learning your weaknesses." She smiled. "The impatience you have for her to be up and moving. The impudence you show in not giving her credit for taking care of business. She's learning you, Stoddard, and before this op is over, she's going to be pulling more strings than you even thought she knew about."

"I don't think so," Stoddard said. No one knew every string he had to pull. No one ever did.

"If someone plays with you long enough," Corbin promised, "you reveal more than you think you do. You're clever, but you forget other people are clever, too."

For just the barest moment, Stoddard viewed the young

agent's words as a veiled threat. Then he dismissed the anger stirring inside him. This was his game. He'd designed the play piece by piece. No one else could even come close. But he checked the impulse to say something in response.

Saengkeo Zhao had just gone on the move.

9

Saengkeo Zhao strode into the HSBC Building with her head high and tried to ignore the whisper of dread that echoed at the back of her mind. When the structure was constructed back in 1985, the Hongkong and Shanghai Banking Corporation Building was—at 5.2 billion in Hong Kong dollars—the most expensive building in the world. The building was designed to both impress and intimidate.

Entering the building with guards on either side of her, Saengkeo scanned the people milling around the first floor. No threat was apparent, but she knew Stoddard would be watching her. Doubtless, Yang would be watching, as well. And perhaps there would be other triad leaders and warlords taking part in the observations.

She felt like a canary in a glass cage. The feeling was furthered by the huge atrium inside the building. From first glance, the structure appeared to be made almost entirely of glass. Huge steel girders shot skyward to hold the slanted roof above, while other beams crisscrossed between them, looking like giant steel butterflies anchored to the structure. Offices lined the atrium area in neat layers, leaving the space open in the center of the building except for the steel butterfly support beams.

She crossed the foyer, the bodyguards in perfect step around her, and headed for the escalator leading to the first floor. Security cameras monitored the ebb and flow of people into and out of the building, and she knew not all of them belonged to the HSBC security teams. Some of them, in fact, were ones she'd paid to have the use of.

"We must talk," Johnny Kwan said.

"Yes," she replied. The radio connection came from a tiny device in her ear. The device was both receiver and transmitter, and didn't prevent her from hearing normal noises around her. The device picked up a signal and translated the electronic data to words so she could hear them. As a transmitter, the device picked up her own speech through the bones in her jaw and her ear canal, and broadcast them to other devices on the same band. Despite the visible concealment and the difficulty in pinpointing who might be using the frequency, she knew that the signal—and the conversation—could be monitored.

"I will be joining you in a moment."

"Here?" Saengkeo's heartbeat sped a little. The plan was for Kwan to stay apart from her and manage the exfiltration teams if such an avenue became necessary.

"I have news you need," Kwan stated evenly.

The news wasn't about the HSBC Building or the coming confrontation, Saengkeo knew. Otherwise Kwan would have advised her to break off the engagement. The only news Kwan might be carrying was about Pei-Ling Bao or the address the CIA agent had given her.

"Now?" Saengkeo asked.

"If I did not think so," Kwan replied in a neutral voice that still spoke volumes about his disapproval of her need to ask such a question, "I would not bring the news to you."

"Of course." Saengkeo kept contriteness from her voice. Syn-Tek dealt with Kwan's directness so much better than she did.

Kwan joined her at the foot of the escalator. He carried a palm-size DVD player in his hand.

When the device was offered, Saengkeo took the DVD player and the thick-lensed, wraparound sunglasses Kwan offered. The sunglasses held microcircuitry in the slender frames. She plugged the coaxial cable that hung from one of the sunglasses earpieces into the DVD player and pressed Play.

The opaque quality of the sunglasses severely limited her vision. When the coaxial cable transmitted the DVD player's program, she no longer saw the HSBC Building at all.

Smoothly and with the correct amount of politeness because Johnny Kwan was a samurai in his own mind, Kwan took Saengkeo's elbow and guided her as if she were blind. She trusted his lead implicitly as they stepped from the escalator. Kwan knew the way to the meeting offices as well as she did. He'd been there several times with Syn-Tek.

The image on the projection lenses of the sunglasses showed the inside of a small warehouse. Inside the warehouse was a sleek, fast cigarette boat. The vessel was a smuggler's tool, built for speed and possessing limited cargo space, but the only cargo the boat carried was strictly high-dollar merchandize.

"This is at the address I gave you?" Saengkeo asked.

"Yes." Kwan pulled at her elbow slightly.

Saengkeo followed without hesitation. She watched as the

views flickered and changed, rotating all around the boat. The picture changed a few times as bright spots appeared on the screen and illuminated dozens of bullet holes that had ripped through the vessel's fiberglass body. "You took pictures?"

"No. We hacked into the security system watching over the boat. The boathouse is too heavily guarded. Until I conferred with you, I didn't want to do anything."

"Is there anything else on the DVD?"

"Only that. We intercepted the signal, then burned a copy for you."

Saengkeo removed the sunglasses, blinking rapidly for a moment at the brightness of the day. She handed the DVD player and the glasses back to Kwan.

Still holding her politely by the elbow, Kwan guided her toward a bank of elevators. As smoothly as though the pickup up had been arranged at that precise moment, one of Kwan's handpicked team members folded his book and started toward them.

The man was young, dressed in casual clothing and never once looked at Saengkeo or Kwan. He took the proffered DVD disk from Kwan with the skill of a trained pickpocket. Another disk gleamed in Kwan's hand for an instant, then found a home in the DVD player. Saengkeo doubted anyone had seen the exchange.

That was Kwan: always a step ahead and planning for everything.

Even as the man's attention to detail registered on her, Saengkeo couldn't help but think that Kwan wasn't there for Syn-Tek when he'd needed him most. Her brother had died without his friend and right-hand man. A paranoid thought ghosted through her mind, making her wonder just for a moment if Kwan had planned that absence.

Saengkeo steered her thoughts from that path and concentrated on what she faced. The men she'd be meeting in only moments were deadly and greedy.

"What do you want to do about the boat?" Kwan asked.

"Have you identified the vessel?"

"Again, I waited for your decision regarding the matter."

"There was identification?"

"Yes."

"That identification could be false."

Kwan nodded. "That identification could also be a trap. The surveillance system we hacked into was constructed of British equipment, but the setup was American."

"You're certain?"

Kwan shrugged. "With enough time spent on these things, you get a feeling about them."

"Of course. You fear betrayal."

"Not fear betrayal. I expect it so that I will never be truly surprised." Kwan regarded her with his night-black eyes. "As should you."

"Even from you?"

For a moment, Kwan's face remained stony. Then a brief smile flickered at the corner of his lips. "Even from me."

"This wasn't the only thing that brought you to me now," Saengkeo said.

"No. I have received further news."

"About?"

"The girl."

Her heart fluttered, but she stilled the emotion inside herself. She became the quiet pool that Ea-Han had taught her to do all those years ago. "Does she live?"

"As far as I know."

"Where is she?"

"Perhaps she is where we were told she would be." Kwan spoke obliquely so that the security devices could tape his conversation and still learn nothing. "I am working on the problem now."

"You will let me know?"

"Immediately."

"Then what news have you learned?"

"There was another triad inquiring about her arrival," Kwan said.

"Who?"

"The Green Ghosts."

Saengkeo thought back, having a little difficulty placing the triad. "New York City."

"Yes."

"Did she pass through there?"

"No."

"Then how would they know of her?"

"Because the Russian *mafiya* knew of her."

Saengkeo studied on the problem for a moment. The situation made no sense. "We have no dealings with the Russian *mafiya* or the Green Ghost triad."

"No," Kwan agreed.

Saengkeo hesitated. "Did my brother?"

"No. He would have told you."

"And yet, there is much that he did not tell me."

Kwan's silence was damning. He didn't look at her.

"There is much you haven't told me," Saengkeo accused.

"Yes."

"When will you?"

"When it is time," Kwan said.

Saengkeo stared at the man. "You spoke only moments ago of my needing to expect betrayal from even you. Is your refusal to answer part of such a betrayal?"

"No," Kwan answered. "In this, I follow Syn-Tek's wishes."

"And there are things that my brother would not have wanted me to know?"

"Of course," Kwan said. "You were his sister, not his brother. There are things that a man doesn't want even his sister to know."

"I don't believe that."

Kwan looked at her. "Did your brother know all of your business, Saengkeo? About the men you were with? About the way you used your power in this family?"

For a moment, Saengkeo held the man's eyes. What Kwan said was true. There was a lot that Syn-Tek hadn't known about her life. They had been in the United States at different times because their father had never wanted to chance losing them both at the same time. The benefits of a Western education to complete their schooling—especially in light of their grand plan for the Moon Shadow family—couldn't be ignored.

She hadn't been a virgin when she'd gone to the United States, but after she'd arrived there, she'd been no stranger to men. That was part of her life. She hadn't loved often or long, but she had taken brief harbor in the arms of men willing to share their lives for a short time. She'd left broken hearts behind, as well as two stalkers. One was dead at the hands of others, and one she'd killed herself when he'd followed her to Paris. Neither her father nor Syn-Tek knew of those experiences.

"No," Saengkeo admitted reluctantly.

"Then let me honor this," Kwan said, "Syn-Tek's last request, in death as I honored him in life."

"Of course. Forgive me for asking." But Saengkeo's mind couldn't keep from pulling at the knowledge she already had, trying to piece the facts together to find out what Kwan hid from her. Only the fact that whatever the secret was had to have shamed Syn-Tek remained.

And if that secret had shamed her brother, Saengkeo knew that learning the truth would probably hurt her. She steeled herself.

"How did the Russian *mafiya* know of the girl?" she asked as they circled the concourse to the elevators on the other side of the HSBC Building.

"From the Green Ghosts. The *mafiya* was buying the information from the Green Ghosts."

"Why?"

Kwan shrugged.

Saengkeo watched him, knowing that the man's reticence came from protecting part of Syn-Tek's secret. A memory floated unbidden to the top of her mind. "I heard a rumor just a few days ago."

"Rumors are not always trustworthy things."

"No, and that was why I dismissed the rumor so casually. But I was told that the Russian *mafiya* was setting up a deal for nuclear arms with a terrorist group in the Middle East, and that they were planning to traffic the deal through Chinese territories."

Kwan shook his head. "You can hear any number of things if you listen for them. The Americans constantly live under the fear of nuclear attack. Their spy agencies foster those fears to keep money flowing into their departments."

"I heard the nuclear arms were from the Russian submarine that sank so tragically not long ago."

Kwan shrugged again, then gestured toward the elevators just ahead of them.

Three men in black suits held the crowd of tourists and business people at bay. The men were polite but firm and insistent. All of them belonged to Johnny Kwan.

Kwan guided Saengkeo to the elevator cage. Several men and women looked at Kwan with irritation and challenge in their gazes. All of them quickly looked away if they happened to catch his eye.

Saengkeo entered the elevator cage, but Kwan remained outside. He leaned in close after her, then whispered, "There has been a further problem in New York City."

Saengkeo waited.

"The Italian Mafia has taken an interest, as well," Kwan said. "There was a man the Green Ghosts speak of. A very dangerous man."

"Who is he?"

Kwan shook his head. "A Black Ace. He calls himself Frank Lambretta."

Saengkeo recognized the term. Black Aces were high in the hierarchy of the American and Italian organized crime Families. "Why would this man be interested in what is going on in New York City?"

"I don't know. But he left a lot of dead men behind him. Some of them, as it turns out, had connections with the American CIA."

"Does our contact know?" Saengkeo asked, referring to Stoddard.

"I don't know what he knows," Kwan admitted. "The media has been keeping the story quiet. Since the Afghanistan war, the Americans have wanted to tout the CIA as heroes."

Saengkeo knew that. She also knew that not all heroes remained heroes or acted only as heroes would act. And honor and duty were things affected by perception, and tools used by those that would manipulate men of honor.

"How did you learn of the CIA connection?" Saengkeo asked.

"We Moon Shadows," Kwan explained, "are noted for our generosity regarding those who help us. The Green Ghosts are not noted for keeping too many secrets because they are constantly selling themselves to one buyer or another. Finding out these things was a relatively small matter. But knowing where to look was only good fortune."

Saengkeo looked at the man. Johnny Kwan was one of the last people in the world who would talk about good fortune being responsible for something.

"If you need me," Kwan promised, "I'm here."

"Of course you are," Saengkeo acknowledged.

Kwan inclined his head and released the elevator doors. He remained standing in her view until the doors closed. A moment later, the cage vaulted for the upper floors.

When the elevator arrived at its destination, Saengkeo was once more focused, the disturbing enigma of the cigarette boat in the warehouse at the address Stoddard had given her now at the back of her mind.

Sunlight glinted from the cross beams, but the light never quite fell directly on the walkway. Saengkeo drew stares from the various security men stationed at that level. Over thirty triad heads were attending the meeting. Other triad leaders, those currently held in disfavor by the Chinese government or wanted for criminal activities, would be there via teleconferencing. The video and audio sat links were supposed to be heavily encrypted and secure, but that only meant the common street criminals wouldn't know what took place.

United Bamboo and the Big Circle Society held the rights to the front door and served as hosts for the event. Their security people were deadly earnest about their jobs.

Saengkeo held her arms up, hands crossed behind her head, as a two-man team ran a security wand over her. Hands followed next, circumspect but thorough. She didn't feel entirely violated when they finished and waved her through.

Once through the gauntlet and standing in the open throat

of the hallway beyond the checkpoint, Saengkeo stood and waited while the security team dealt with her bodyguards. They took more time with the two men. The bodyguards never moved, never acknowledged the touch of the men searching them.

The security team gave up their efforts at length. They looked disappointed that they hadn't found anything on the men. Saengkeo had known the men would check out. Johnny Kwan had assured her of that, just as he had assured her that the two men would be among the most deadly in the room. Saengkeo didn't doubt that, either.

The hallway continued for a short distance, then curved to the right. Modular walls formed the hallway. Traditional Chinese lute music filled the hallway.

"Miss Zhao," a thin, well-dressed man announced as she neared the final set of doors.

The maître d' appeared English, not Chinese, and she wondered if he knew that he had been deliberately chosen for his heritage. Then she decided that whether he knew wasn't important. More than anything else, she knew the man would be well paid, and the standards that he had to adhere to would be exacting.

He smiled easily, obviously awaiting her reaction.

"Yes," Saengkeo acknowledged.

"It is a pleasure to serve you, Miss Zhao," the thin man said. "My name is Henry. Should you need anything, my staff and I will be most thankful if you would just let us know."

"I will."

"If I may, miss..." Henry extended a small notebook with gilt lettering scrolled across the front.

Saengkeo took the notebook.

"That's your itinerary, Miss Zhao," Henry declared. "The itinerary notes everything that will be covered in the meeting, and during what times. Intermissions are scheduled on a regular basis."

Saengkeo flipped through the itinerary, amazed at how thorough the document was. Police agencies around the world, she realized, would have given much to get their hands on a copy.

"When you leave the meeting, Miss Zhao," Henry went on, "you'll be expected to return all written materials." He seemed a little nervous.

"Of course," Saengkeo said, closing the notebook. She gave the man a small smile. Henry appeared exceedingly nervous. For a moment she wondered if Yang had been talking and if the small, dapper Englishman had heard she was responsible for the explosion out in Victoria Harbour. Despite the fact that no one from the Hong Kong Police Department had yet come calling, Saengkeo was grimly aware that she might not have heard the end of the matter.

And she was certain that Yang wasn't yet done with the situation.

Henry snapped his fingers imperiously. One of the impeccably attired servers standing behind him stepped forward.

"This way, Miss Zhao," the server said.

Saengkeo fell into step behind the man. He led her through double doors into a large banquet area. Red linen covered the small, intimate tables. The chairs were black lacquer, carved with dragon heads in bas-relief. Red-and-black wooden tiles covered the floor, and they hadn't been the original floor covering. The meeting had been well planned and well funded.

As she crossed the room, Saengkeo realized that she knew most of the men in attendance. At least, she knew the important ones. Many new faces were also in evidence, men who had been promoted up through the ranks after their predecessors were killed or executed. The triads always had job openings for honest men willing to die violently and suddenly.

The floor had also been altered to allow different sections to be raised above the others. Status was central to triad life, and no bones were made about that fact. A long table at the head of the room was the highest of all. Only the most important men, triad heads of United Bamboo and the Big Circle Society, would sit there.

And that was only for this day. By next week, the two largest triads in China and around the world could be at each other's throats again. The day after that happened, all of the lesser triads would be expected to choose one organization over the other.

A momentary feeling of satisfaction passed through Saengkeo as the server led her to one of the tables of medium height and nearer the main table than most. The table occupied a place of honor and interest between the two large triads.

The server pulled out the seat and Saengkeo sat. She was conscious of the stares of the men. Only a few women were in attendance at the meeting. Discreetly, Saengkeo glanced at the women, each in turn. Most of them were bodyguards, but a few were triad lieutenants. None of them represented a triad family as she did.

Saengkeo offended the men because she held a position of power, and because she'd chosen not to dress as women were expected at such functions. By rights, she should have been wearing a dress and fawning for the attention of the men.

Her bodyguards took seats on either side of her.

Glancing out over the floor, Saengkeo noted that Yang's table was near the back and at floor level. She took small pleasure in that, as well. The server offered drinks. The body-guards took nothing, not willing to risk being drugged while they kept watch over her. She asked for and received bottled water, not wanting to take any chances, but not wanting to offend her hosts, either.

Five minutes passed. The buzz of conversation filled the room. Da-Xia Huang stepped away from his table and approached her.

Huang was short and heavy. His suit jacket button strained over his girth. A smile was on his round, freshly shaved face. He was in his early fifties and his hair was iron gray with black streaks. He was head of the Red Lightning triad, one of the most aggressive drug-dealing families in the Hong Kong area, with connections that reached into Thailand and Macao. The Red Lightnings also served much of the Holly-wood crowd in Los Angeles, as well as providing drugs to movie crews on location around the world.

"Ah, Saengkeo," Huang greeted her with false warmth, of-fering his hand, English fashion.

Saengkeo ignored the proffered hand, choosing instead to duck her head in a quasibow.

Recovering his aplomb after being dismissed so bluntly, Huang drew his hand back uncertainly and bowed. "As well traveled as you are," the man said, "I didn't know whether to greet you as a woman of our culture or one of the Western world."

Saengkeo knew Huang's words were designed as an insult. "I am Chinese," Saengkeo said in a flat voice. "First, last and always. The daughter of my parents, who knew only the earth, sea and wind of this place." She paused. "And for future reference, Mr. Huang, the matter of shaking hands is always left up to the women even in Western Culture. If you are going to borrow from that culture, make certain you first understand the traditions."

Spots of color shone on Huang's cheeks.

Saengkeo remained seated, using her gender against him. In traditional Chinese society, she would have been ignored for the most part. Women were nothing, only one step removed from chattel even in these so-called enlightened times. But as head of the Moon Shadow triad, respect had to be shown to her.

That fact bothered Huang. She could see the disgust in every line of his body. To make matters worse, he had to discuss personal business with her.

"May I join you?" Huang asked.

"That is not possible," Saengkeo replied. "If you were to sit with me, others in this room might think our business interests were aligned."

Huang tried a smile that didn't quite fit. "I thought our business interests shared common goals."

"No. I am here, in part, to speak on behalf of the Aberdeen fishermen your people have been threatening."

The Red Lightning triad leader's face hardened as if covered by a layer of shellac. "Those people are none of your concern."

Saengkeo picked up the chopsticks by her plate. She twisted the slim wooden sticks in her hands as she returned Huang's challenging glare full measure. "Those fishermen are under the protection of the Moon Shadow family."

Huang shrugged. "Perhaps we are talking about two different sets of fishermen."

"No," Saengkeo said. "I'm talking about the Aberdeen fishermen that sail for legitimate canneries my family owns. Your raiders have been stealing young people from them, boys who have been put to work on ships you own, and young women that have been forced into prostitution in the brothels you own."

Uneasiness showed on Huang's face. "Surely you have me confused with someone else. I'm certain that if you investigate the matter further—"

"I have investigated the matter further," Saengkeo interrupted. She knew that their exchange had stilled many of the conversations around them. Other conversations lurched to a halt as the confrontation claimed an even larger audience. "I know that your men have been the ones guilty of raiding the fishing community. My brother had warned you of your transgressions, and he told you the penalty he would exact."

Anger flared through Huang and narrowed his pupils to pinpricks. He placed his left hand on the table and leaned across, jabbing at Saengkeo with his right forefinger. "Your brother is dead, and I'll not suffer to be threatened by a bitch who would be better used servicing men as a common—"

Saengkeo saw her own bodyguards rising from their seats. They moved a little uncertainly because Huang was an important man and because he hadn't yet physically touched her. Even Huang's own men came forward, but they looked prepared to stop their employer.

Cold satisfaction filled Saengkeo. She leaned forward before Huang could move and took a chopstick in each hand. With a swift, economical movement, she drove the chopstick in her right hand through Huang's left hand on the table. Blood blossomed on the back of his hand as she pinned him there. Even as he started to scream in pain, Saengkeo rose lithely, bent her left arm and caught Huang's throat in the crook of her elbow.

Her strength and speed and anger, as well as the placement of the table, allowed her to bend the Red Lightning triad leader over the table, throwing him to his back. She thrust the chopstick in her left hand under Huang's chin, pressing the end against the soft flesh of the man's throat. The flesh gave way and a bright drop of blood appeared.

Huang's bodyguards recovered from their stunned surprise and rushed forward.

10

"Son of a bitch!" David Kelso exploded. "She's going to get herself killed."

Rance Stoddard gazed at the two monitors that showed the potentially lethal encounter taking place in the HSBC Building. For a moment, he truly believed Saengkeo Zhao had taken leave of her senses. Unconsciously, the CIA section chief toggled the joystick, centering the two button cameras his team had planted in the room on the woman and the man she held captive.

"Stay back!" Saengkeo ordered.

The two bodyguards approaching her stopped. If they'd had weapons, Stoddard was certain they would have shot her dead.

"If you come any closer," Saengkeo threatened in a cold voice, "I'm going to spear his throat, and you can watch him drown in his own blood."

"Son of a bitch," Kelso repeated in awe. He sat on the corner of the desk.

A lighter snapped.

Stoddard craned his head around and gazed at Jacy Corbin sitting calmly in one of the overstuffed executive chairs.

Corbin inhaled the cigarette smoke and casually crossed her legs. She smiled, but the emotion never touched her eyes, then released a stream of blue-gray smoke. "I've got to tell you, the woman is beginning to impress the hell out of me."

"Maybe she just knows we're watching," Stoddard suggested. He made the statement calm, although his heart pounded his rib cage. Part of his mind was already occupied with cutting his losses on Saengkeo Zhao's involvement. Maybe the Moon Shadow triad had weighed in heavily enough. But he knew that wasn't true. There were still two Russian nuclear warheads to be accounted for.

Corbin shook her head. "No way. For this, she thinks she's on her own, and she's betting the house. What you're looking at there, gentlemen, is sheer guts. It's all or nothing for her. She's my kind of woman."

The tension in the HSBC Building banquet room continued. With the other camera, Stoddard tracked the rest of the room, watching as a few of the men retreated into one of the hallways leading away from the conference area. The CIA agent hated the trapped, useless feeling that cascaded inside him.

"Who is the man?" Stoddard asked. He checked the name he'd written on the small legal pad beside the keyboard. Some old habits and methods of doing things died hard.

"Da-Xia Huang," Jacy answered. "Family head of the Red Lightning triad."

"He's not a major player."

"Maybe not," Corbin agreed. "But today he is."

"What is his connection to Saengkeo?"

Corbin grinned at Stoddard, and he realized that his use of the woman's first name was going to be remembered.

"He's been poaching on Moon Shadow territory," the woman agent said. "Just like Saengkeo laid it out. The Aberdeen fishermen have been loyal to the Moon Shadow family for the past hundred years or so. Even before Jik-Chang Zhao moved the core of the family from Shanghai to Hong Kong. Huang has been boarding the fishing boats and taking people from them."

"Syn-Tek Zhao knew about this?" Stoddard asked.

"Yes."

"I don't recall the discussion."

"His problems," Corbin pointed out, "weren't necessarily your problems. And he knew there was a limit to how much the Agency would get involved in a triad turf war." She paused. "As an added bonus, Saengkeo may believe that Huang had her brother murdered."

"My name is Saengkeo Zhao," the woman said, maintaining her hold on her captive. "I am family head of the Moon Shadow triad."

Stoddard watched the monitor as Saengkeo raked the rest of the banquet room with a challenging stare. She was, he had to admit, nothing short of incredible. But she was also one short step away from sudden death.

Glancing at Kelso, Stoddard said, "Get over there. Take command of the field agents and keep me apprised of the situation."

"By the time I get over there," Kelso said, "it could all be over. One way or another."

"Do it."

Reluctantly Kelso nodded. "Burn a DVD. I hate leaving at the good parts."

Stoddard ignored the request. DVDs were already being burned for use in identifying the various Asian crime lords. Many of them had business in the United States, as well as within the intelligence sectors these days. With the advent of technology and the importance of the world economy, the intelligence sectors were distinctly linked to national profit-and-loss statements.

"This man has harmed people who entrusted their care to me," Saengkeo continued, "and he has disrespected me. If I so choose, his life is forfeit to me. Many of you have never met me. Some of you might not even know who I am." She kept her grip on the two chopsticks. Huang's injured hand trembled as she held the chopstick pinned to the table. She felt his jugular beating against the chopstick she held in her other hand.

The two men Johnny Kwan had assigned to protect her stood on either side of her in martial-arts stances. They formed a living flesh-and-blood barrier between her and the rest of the room. Huang's own bodyguards stood at bay.

"Saengkeo," Johnny Kwan spoke through the ear transceiver she wore, "you must stop. This is madness."

No, Saengkeo thought. Her behavior wasn't madness. Syn-Tek's death was madness, and she felt certain that someone in the room had killed her brother or ordered his death. She felt Huang cough, choking a little on the chopstick pressed so tightly against his throat.

"For a long time," Saengkeo said, "the Moon Shadow family has been nonaggressive. We have pursued a peaceful path to build our family's future. That ended the day my brother was murdered."

Murmurs filled the room. Saengkeo doubted that Syn-Tek's death was news to anyone, but there might have been some from outside Hong Kong or Asia that might not have known.

"Do you know what you are saying?" Kwan asked over the transceiver. "You are issuing a challenge to these people. And you are a woman, Saengkeo. They will not take this easily."

Saengkeo kept focused on the crowd in the banquet room. These people she faced had no other choice except to take what she had to say.

"No more will the Moon Shadows turn a blind eye to the encroachment of other families," Saengkeo promised. "We will hold the empire my family has built, and we will strike out at those that transgress against us."

A group of men walked into the room from the hallway behind the main table. Some of those men were in their eighties, but their eyes still held intelligence and cruel ambition. They regarded her stoically, as if realizing that she wouldn't stop until she had her say.

Or maybe they realized that she would have killed Huang to prove her point. Even in the HSBC Building with the controls they had in place, United Bamboo and the Big Circle Society heads would be hard-pressed to keep secret the news of someone's death inside the structure.

The Chinese government officials standing with the triad heads definitely didn't want the attention. Their interest in Afghanistan reparations, the oil industry in the Middle East and the ongoing conflict with Taiwan heating up again was well-documented by the Western world. Getting caught in such a debacle would fuel media for weeks and would cause political and economic backlashes throughout China that would be fueled by the Western media.

"Miss Zhao," Min-Soo Luo called from the head table. He was bespectacled and as thin as a famine victim. Despite his tailor's attentions, his black suit hung on him. His hair was dyed black and laid back in strands so thin they showed his scalp. A short mustache shadowed his upper lip. He was one of the most prominent leaders of the United Bamboo triad present at the meeting.

Saengkeo looked at the man.

"I would prefer," Luo stated, "that you don't kill Huang or even further damage him."

"Huang has damaged people who have entrusted their care to me," Saengkeo said. "My brother would not have stood for the things Huang has done in these past weeks since his death. I will not stand for them, either."

"My family still has use for Huang and the Red Lightning triad."

"As you wish," Saengkeo acknowledged. "If you find this man of worth to you, then I won't harm him." She turned back to Huang and saw the faint flicker of hope in the man's eyes. "But I promise you this—if he dares again to treat me or anyone in my family, or under the protection of my family, with anything less than respect, I will hunt him down and kill him. Is this acceptable, Master Luo?"

The old man hesitated for a moment.

"Damn it, Saengkeo," Kwan said over the transceiver, "you dare too much. You can't back Luo against the wall and not expect him to react."

Saengkeo held the chopstick against her captive's jugular. She was only a fraction of an inch from spilling Huang's blood and taking his life. Everyone in the room knew that, and none doubted her. She saw the belief burning in the eyes of the audience.

"The arrangement," Luo said slowly, "is acceptable."

"Then I give you back the life of this worthless person," Saengkeo said, choosing her words with care so that they echoed polite formality while at the same time heaping insult to Huang. "I know that you will make better use of his life than he has sense to make of the years himself."

A small, cold grin fitted Luo's wrinkled face. "Yes." He waved to Saengkeo.

Trembling inside but steeling herself not to show the emotion on the outside, Saengkeo took the chopstick away from Huang's throat. She stepped back from the Red Lightning triad leader, then yanked free the chopstick impaled in Huang's hand.

Huang yelped in pain and dropped to his knees. He clutched his injured hand to him. His bodyguards started toward him, but Saengkeo froze them in place with a single glance. They had no choice but to believe she would go after them next. Then, after the space of a breath, she stepped back.

The older bodyguard nodded to Saengkeo in deference while the other gazed at her with white-hot anger. Together, they picked up Huang from the floor and walked with the man's arms pulled across their shoulders.

"Miss Zhao," Luo said, "it seems as though you have disrupted this meeting."

"For that," Saengkeo said, "I humbly apologize. I had no way of knowing that Huang would treat me with such disrespect."

"Perhaps. But I have also heard that you have a temper."

"Whoever told you that," Saengkeo said, "told you wrong. Would you have the head of a triad that you seek to do business with treated so badly at your meeting?"

Luo remained silent.

"I acted," Saengkeo said with conviction, "only as I perceived you would have acted if you had known." She lifted her chin then, meeting the old man's gaze. "I am not just a woman, Master Luo. I am the head of the Moon Shadow triad, and I will demand the honor and respect that is due me by my birthright, as well as the blood my ancestors have shed to earn those things." She bowed, never taking her eyes from his, knowing the whole time that Luo's guards at least would be armed. She hovered only a heartbeat from death.

For a moment, silence hung heavily in the banquet room.

Then Luo glanced at her. "Well spoken, Miss Zhao. You defend your family's honor with all the zeal and efficiency of your brother and your father. A very noble effort on your part." He looked away from her, then around at the group. "While she remains an invited guest of United Bamboo, no one will raise a hand against Miss Zhao or that person will suffer the wrath of my family."

No one said anything.

Luo turned toward Saengkeo and held out his hand. "Come, Miss Zhao. Tonight you will share my table. If that is amenable to you."

Surprised, Saengkeo found herself at a loss for words for a moment. "Of course, Master Luo. Thank you on behalf of my family for your generosity."

Uniformed servers hurried to set another place at the long table.

As Saengkeo took her place at the table, accepting Luo's offer to pull out her chair, she knew that in the past few moments she had changed the mix of the meeting. Most of the triad heads wouldn't have thought twice about her before today, but the story of Min-Soo Luo's recognition of her, coupled with stories of the confrontation with Wai-Lim Yang and the sinking of *Goldfish* in Victoria Harbour, would set tongues to wagging.

People would hear of her, and they would hear of the Moon Shadow triad. Her father would never have approved of the family running such a high profile. But Saengkeo knew she had no choice if she was to save her family more quickly. And if she was to find her brother's killer.

"Very good," Johnny Kwan whispered into her ear over the transceiver.

And though she'd succeeded past anything she might have imagined, Saengkeo didn't allow herself to relax. In truth, she'd stepped closer to death than ever before.

Arizona

MACK BOLAN SAT behind the wheel of the rental SUV and surveyed the bar he'd staked out two hours ago. The local time was now 1:13 a.m., and the Desert Heat Nightclub was doing booming business.

Neon lights blistered the night, spewing from the sign atop the single-story dance club a couple blocks off North Scottsdale Road. The area was the main nightlife drag in Scottsdale, Arizona. Gravel covered the parking area, popping and snapping as cars passed through.

The club attracted mostly a young male clientele, drawn no doubt by the neon figurine of the miniskirted figure doing a Marilyn Monroe *The Seven-Year Itch* imitation over and over again in an endless loop. For those who couldn't understand the simple medium of hieroglyphics advertising the promise of sex, the marquee announced Live Nude Girls. A heavy basso beat from subwoofers pumped up on electronic steroids rolled over the parking area.

Seven minutes later, the white Cadillac Bolan had been waiting on rolled into the parking area. Quietly, combat senses alert, the Executioner visually tagged the men getting out of the car.

Two hard-bodied guys got out of the front and swept the parking lot with their gaze. Both men were broad and both moved with economical grace that spoke of time spent in martial-arts dojos. They walked to the back of the vehicle and opened both doors.

Rudolpho Garcia stepped from the back seat. He was a couple of years short of the thirty-year mark, but he'd spent over half that time involved with career crime. When he'd been younger, Garcia had been a smash-and-grab guy. A jolt in an Arizona boys' home teamed him up with a couple of other guys his age who gave him training in residential boosts. That had carried him until his eighteenth year, when he'd gravitated to rape and home robbery. Only the B&E had been proved, and he took a three-year fall. During that term, he'd become something of an artist, specializing in fake documentation for Mexican and Chinese illegal aliens. He'd nearly taken a couple more falls involving local hotel chains that had gotten fined for falsifying workers' records.

Bolan had gotten Garcia's name and probable whereabouts from the files Barbara Price had forwarded from Stony Man Farm. Once he'd read the guy's jacket, the soldier had known Garcia might have access to the information and weapons he needed.

Garcia wore designer jeans, a pearl-snap cowboy shirt and a fringed black-and-white-cowhide jacket. Silver glinted around the crown of his cowboy hat. He was taller than his guard, nearly six and a half feet tall, with broad shoulders and narrow hips. Large Mexican-roweled spurs jutted from his hand-tooled boots. He had slitted eyes and a thin gunfighter mustache.

A small brunette clad in a short, too tight black cocktail dress that revealed nearly all of her cleavage got out on the other side of the car. Ruby highlights glinted at her ears beneath the short-cropped hair. The club didn't allow anyone inside less than twenty years of age. Bolan doubted the girl had seen eighteen yet.

Garcia took the lead, flanked by the girl and one of the bodyguards while the other man went to park the car.

Bolan eased out from behind the rental vehicle's wheel and fell in behind Garcia and his entourage. The soldier paid the cover charge and passed into the building close on the heels of his quarry.

The club's interior was dark and filled with smoke. Three stages circled the room. Women gyrated on the stages, removing clothing to the overpowering speed-metal beat.

Small tables ringed by chairs filled the center area. Servers in hot pants and club T-shirts advertising Desert Heat threaded through the narrow spaces between the tables. Some of the men got slapped for being too bold as the women passed by.

Bolan counted four guys in black T-shirts marked Desert Heat Security positioned around the room. They were all young, used to handling drunks and would-be troublemakers. None of them were close to the table Garcia and his crew took back by the two pool tables against the far wall.

Making no pretense, Bolan turned and strode for Garcia's table, setting off the man's personal warning system. The Executioner was unarmed. He'd had to ditch his weapons back in New York City before taking the flight out. Part of his reason for seeing Garcia was to rearm himself, but the other part was to gather intel.

Lounging in his chair, right hand tucked into the pocket of his fringed jacket, Garcia stared at Bolan, then nodded to his two bodyguards.

Never breaking stride, the Executioner plucked the pool cue from the hands of one of the nearby players. Swinging the cue by the small end, Bolan landed a vicious blow against the temple of the bodyguard on the left. The cue shattered at the impact, but the man went down, out cold.

Whipping the small piece of pool stick that remained in his hands, Bolan caught the wrist of the second bodyguard's gun hand as he brought a pistol from beneath his coat. The Executioner bent as he stepped forward, then caught the falling pistol in a one-handed scoop. He dodged the awkward straight-off-the-shoulder blow the big man aimed at him, then lifted his foot and stamped down hard against the man's knee.

Bone shattered, popping loudly enough in the nearby area to draw the attention of a few club patrons. The bodyguard mewled in pain and sagged to one side. Still on the move, Bolan swept the bodyguard aside, using the man for defensive cover as Garcia brought out a Colt .45.

Unwilling to kill the man if he didn't have to, Bolan drew the broken length of pool cue back and threw. The shattered cue spun once, then the broken end slammed into Garcia's forehead. The guy's head snapped backward. Before his quarry could recover enough to squeeze his weapon's trigger, the Executioner caught the .45 in his hand, prevented the pistol from firing by bracing his thumb against the hammer and twisted, wrenching away the .45.

"Bastard!" Garcia swore, staring up at Bolan from the mask of blood that covered his face. The pool cue shard had lacerated his forehead.

The girl screamed, pushing herself back and away frantically.

Bolan let the girl go. If she'd have been armed, she'd have brought the weapon into play. He turned his attention to Garcia.

"Get up," Bolan ordered.

The crowd around them fanned out, trying to stay out of the line of fire but remaining spectators all the same.

"Fuck you, man," Garcia snarled. "Show me a badge."

Without a word, Bolan stepped forward.

Garcia rose suddenly, obviously thinking Bolan wouldn't fire. The man flipped the table up as a barricade. The Executioner drove a foot into the table, sending it back into Garcia and knocking the man down. Before Garcia could push himself up, Bolan gripped a fistful of fringed cowhide jacket and cowboy shirt and lifted the man from the floor.

Garcia tried desperately to kick his attacker, but Bolan stayed in close, turning so the kicks slid along his thighs and hips without doing any damage. The Executioner kept his quarry moving, driving him back between a pair of pool tables and sending players scurrying. He kept Garcia moving, kept the man off balance and slammed him against the back wall. Garcia's head hit the wall with a distinct thud. Blood continued to pour down his face from the wound on his forehead.

Catching movement in his peripheral vision, Bolan turned and lifted the captured Colt .45 pistol in his fist. He centered the weapon on the bar bouncer's chest.

The bouncer froze and lifted his hands.

"This isn't any of your business," Bolan said. He maintained his hold on Garcia's jacket, shoving the man up against the wall.

"Right," the bouncer said. "I don't want any of the straights hurt."

"Not if they don't deal themselves in," Bolan promised. He wouldn't have hurt bystanders anyway, but his words carried enough warning to any of the men who might have drunk enough to play hero.

Another bouncer joined the first, but held up when the first bouncer told him to stay back.

Bolan released his hold on Garcia, then caught the man's shoulder and flipped him around. The soldier took a fresh grip on Garcia's jacket collar and screwed the .45's barrel into the back of the man's neck with bruising force.

"Back door," Bolan ordered. "Let's go."

Reluctantly, Garcia went. "Who are you, man?"

Bolan ignored the question and kept Garcia moving. The club crowd followed at a discreet distance, but no one attempted to intervene.

"Fuck you, man," Garcia growled. "I ain't afraid of you." But he was. Fear showed in his eyes and echoed in his voice.

"Be afraid," Bolan advised as he shoved his captive through the club's back door. Outside, he pushed Garcia to the right, aiming for the parking lot in front of the building.

"Did somebody send you to do this?" Garcia's tough-guy image started to fall apart. "I got money. I mean, if that's what this shit is all about, I got money. Between you and me, I got enough that whoever's payin' you can't pay you enough to do this, you know."

Conscious of the fact that the Scottsdale PD might be rolling on a call even then, Bolan stepped up the pace, pulling Garcia along in a lockstep. He kept the .45 tight against the side of the man's throat.

"Think about it, you know," Garcia went on. "That's all I'm sayin', man. Just think about it. You kill me, you get a check outta the deal, but you get a murder beef hangin' over your head, too. I pay you, you walk away with no murder beef. Is that a fuckin' deal or what?"

Bolan shoved the man into the passenger seat of the rental SUV. "If you move out of this seat, I'm going to shoot you through the head."

"What have I done to you, man?"

Ignoring the question, Bolan walked around behind the SUV and climbed in. "Hands on the dash. If you move them, I blow your head off and shove you through the door."

Garcia's hands trembled as he placed them on the dash. "Man, I'm tellin' you, you got the wrong guy. There's been some kind of mistake."

"No mistake." Bolan kept the .45 in his left hand, aiming

across his own body at his prisoner, then keyed the ignition. Pulling the transmission into Drive, he rolled out of the parking lot and onto North Scottsdale Road, heading out of town.

"We are we going?"

"Where I want to go," Bolan replied. "I need two things out of you."

"Name them. You got a harsh way of doin' business, but I like a man that don't fuck around a whole lot."

"We're not doing business," Bolan said.

"Okay, that's cool, too. I'm down with that. Call whatever we're doin' whatever you like. As long as I come outta this with a whole skin, I ain't gonna bitch about it, you know."

"I need weapons," Bolan said. "Heavy ordnance." He hadn't been able to swing a weapons drop through Stony Man Farm in time to guarantee him the movement time frame he needed.

"That's cool," Garcia said, nodding. "I know a guy that could arm you against an invadin' army."

"And I want to know about the Chinese illegals coming into the state tonight."

Garcia balked. "That could be a deal breaker, man."

"Wrong answer," Bolan replied.

"These guys bringin' the illegals in? Man, they're dangerous. If they found out I gave them up, I'm dead."

"You're dead if you don't," Bolan promised in a graveyard voice.

11

Hong Kong

Shortly after eight o'clock, Saengkeo Zhao sat in the spacious back seat of a limousine. The luxury car had been a favorite of her father's. More than twenty years old, the limousine was a collector's piece, as well as transportation.

She wore an ear transceiver that connected her with Johnny Kwan's on-site team closing in on the warehouse that held the mystery boat Rance Stoddard had directed her to. The meeting with the other triad members had gone well and lasted longer than she'd believed possible, and new business, as well as old, had been initiated with other triad families. She'd been recognized and favored by the United Bamboo triad, and no one had tried to kill her during or after the meeting, though she was certain that fact would change over the next few days.

"The security systems around the boathouse have been negated," Kwan reported.

"Yes," Saengkeo replied, only to let him know that she had heard him. She'd expected no less. Kwan and his team were experts at voiding electronic security systems.

"We're attempting entry now."

"I will wait here," Saengkeo said, "but I will not be kept waiting."

Kwan made no reply.

Saengkeo knew the man wasn't happy about her involvement with the situation. Kwan had made his feelings abundantly clear about not wanting her along for the infiltration. She'd been just as adamant about going.

Glancing down at the papers she held, Saengkeo traced the boat's ownership through the printed media. A small courtesy light provided to the limousine passengers rendered the pages readable. Although no one would ever be able to prove the matter in a court of law, the boat had ultimately been owned by one of the shell companies that the Moon Shadow triad controlled. The company was in Macao, where Saengkeo's family did business that they didn't want traced by law-enforcement people or by other triads.

And Syn-Tek, her brother, had hidden the boat's existence from her. Saengkeo knew her brother had kept his own secrets about his personal life, but she had never known him to keep business matters from her. A ball of anger and hurt knotted her stomach, and a bubble of sour sickness burst at the back of her throat.

She didn't know why her brother had hidden the boat's existence, but she knew the reason couldn't be good. The only reason that entered her mind was that her brother had been trying to protect her. Perhaps the secret of the boat had been the thing that had gotten Syn-Tek killed.

Quietly, steeling herself, Saengkeo put the papers back in the sealed folder Kwan had couriered to her outside the

HSBC Building. Whatever the reasons her brother had possessed, she would find them. Doing so, she was certain, would lead her to her brother's murderers. After that, there would be retribution.

"The doors are open," Kwan announced. "No one appears to be here."

"I'm on my way." Saengkeo pressed the intercom button linking the passenger section to the chauffeur.

"Yes, miss?" the driver responded, glancing in the rearview mirror.

"Take us in," Saengkeo directed.

The driver nodded and touched the brim of his hat. "Yes, miss."

Saengkeo leaned back in her seat and breathed regularly, keeping herself focused and relaxed. Skillfully, the driver broke the big car out of the holding pattern he'd held the vehicle in since they'd driven from the HSBC Building, weaving through traffic with ease. The man had been her father's driver, and there was no chauffeur she trusted more.

She was dressed in black for the night. Black jeans designed to allow freedom of movement for martial-arts moves, a black turtleneck and a black watch cap. She wore the Walther Model P-990 QPQs in the double shoulder holster rig under an ebony leather rain duster. A belt containing extra magazines rode her slim hips.

The limousine glided through the narrow streets leading to the boathouse occupied by the mysterious cigarette boat. Over the years, much of Hong Kong Island's docks and anchorage had been built and rebuilt. Dredges constantly churned the waters out in Victoria Harbour to keep the port safe for cargo ships, as well as the pleasure cruisers these days. But the section of the harbor where the boathouse was located was older than most of the dockyards and warehouses. Triad families had holdings among the buildings that had been in the organizations for generations.

"Where to, miss?" the limousine driver asked.

"The alley," Saengkeo asked. "The west side of the boat-house."

"Of course, miss." The chauffeur doused his lights and made the course correction.

The alley was narrow and dark. Security lighting, so prevalent among the newer and tourist sections of the harbor, seemed to be a luxury this part of the docks couldn't afford. However, the lack of lighting was deliberate to shroud the criminal activities that took place there. Few Hong Kong police officers would ever investigate the area on their own, and none would ever come alone or without checking with the larger triad heads. Business was business, and some government officials took their cut of those illicit profits.

The limousine slid to a stop in the alley, and Kwan stepped from the darkness. He opened the door and Saengkeo stepped out.

"Was anyone here?" Saengkeo asked.

"No."

"The security systems?"

"Intruder alerts," Kwan confirmed. "As well as the video surveillance I told you about earlier."

"What about audio pickup?" Saengkeo fell into step beside Kwan as they headed for the boathouse's back door.

"There was a separate system," Kwan said. "A redundancy setup. We negated that one in the same manner as we took care of the video linkage. The video feeds transmit the loop we constructed while the audio pickups transmit another loop."

"What about the rest of the security setup?"

Kwan shrugged as he opened the back door. "Antitheft alarms. Motion detectors. Nothing too exotic."

"Someone went to a lot of trouble to make certain they knew when this place was found."

"Perhaps," Kwan suggested, "Syn-Tek had these systems in place to keep people out."

Saengkeo knew there was no refuting the boat's ownership in light of the secret accounts on Macao. "If Syn-Tek had this boat here, why didn't he tell you?"

Kwan had no answer.

"And who did he have monitoring these systems?" Saengkeo persisted.

"I don't know."

Just inside the doorway, Saengkeo stopped and asked Kwan the most dangerous and most hurtful question she could have ever asked him. "Why didn't Syn-Tek trust you with this?"

Kwan regarded her flatly. If he took any personal insult from the question, none showed. "It wasn't a matter of trust. Your brother confided in me about matters he believed I should know about. I was never among the blood-family members."

Saengkeo acknowledged that with a nod of her head. What Kwan said was true, although with the way Syn-Tek and her father treated the man, an outsider would never have believed that. Still, she wondered if Kwan had felt that division between them too sharply. In the past few months, when Syn-Tek had become so secretive, perhaps that division had been felt more sharply than ever. For a moment, she wondered if Kwan could have betrayed her brother. Then she dismissed the idea. She was too tired these days, too strung out.

"You were the second son my father never had, Johnny Kwan," she said. "And you were brother to my brother."

"Thank you."

"I trust you with my life."

"And I would give mine to protect yours," Kwan said. "Just as I would have given my life to protect Syn-Tek if I'd had the chance."

Nearing the boat, Saengkeo noted all the damage the vessel had suffered. Holes and craters showed in the fiberglass hull. Spiderwebbed cracks bled out from those. Judging from all the damage, she thought a miracle had to have taken place to allow the craft to return to a berth.

Saengkeo glanced around the boathouse and saw that Kwan's men had placed heavy black cloth over the windows. "Do you have a light?"

Kwan nodded to one of his men. Immediately the man stepped over to a halogen lamp at the top of a telescoping pole. When he switched on the lamp, the bright light flared over the cigarette boat.

The fiberglass hull was flat black and held none of the metal flakes in the paint that were characteristic of so many similar boats. The color spoke volumes about the craft. The boat couldn't be anything other than a smuggler's tool.

And Syn-Tek owned this boat. My family owned this boat. The certainty of that bothered Saengkeo deeply. She stepped around the boat, taking in the holes in the hull and the abbreviated Plexiglas windscreen.

"These are bullet holes," she announced.

"Yes," Kwan replied. "I also found traces of blood inside the cargo area."

"How much blood?" she asked.

Kwan shrugged. "Enough."

"Did people die on this boat?"

"I don't know. Perhaps."

Saengkeo wanted to ask if Syn-Tek had died on the boat, but she couldn't put that thought into words.

"I don't know," Kwan repeated, as if guessing what she had

been reluctant to voice. "The bullet holes all appear to have been suffered from without. If the craft had been boarded and her crew killed, I think that the invaders would have sunk the boat."

"Then who brought the boat here? And how did Stoddard know the boat was here?"

Kwan shook his head.

"Was there any trace of cargo?" Saengkeo asked.

"None. But perhaps the cargo was taken by the people who cleaned the boat."

"Someone cleaned the boat?"

"Yes. I know a man who was once involved with Hong Kong Police Department forensics. He went over the boat right after we found it. There is no blood remaining aboard the boat. He only found traces of blood, paths where blood had ran."

"Someone cleaned the boat and brought it here," Saengkeo mused. "Yet no one told us of the boat's existence."

"No."

A chill ghosted through Saengkeo. "Whoever did this is not one of our family."

"Or it was someone that Syn-Tek told not to contact us."

"That still doesn't explain how Stoddard knew about the boat and we didn't."

Kwan looked away for a moment, then looked back. "I advised Syn-Tek not to trust this man. He's American, and he has only his agenda in mind. And even worse, he's an American CIA agent. He will betray anyone he wishes to, then blame his false allegiance on a flag and patriotism that serves as a convenience. Those people know no loyalty."

"Stoddard has already done a lot for the Moon Shadow family," Saengkeo pointed out. But she knew she was providing lip service more for herself than for Kwan. With the revelation of the boat, she wanted to remember what Stoddard had done that was good instead of what he might have done regarding Syn-Tek's death.

"Stoddard has only done so with his own goals in mind," Kwan stated.

The transceiver chirped in Saengkeo's ear.

"Kwan," a male voice said.

Kwan tapped the receiver, activating the vocal pickup. "Yes."

"A man approaches."

"Who?"

"The American."

Saengkeo knew from the tone that there could only be one American. Kwan looked at her, and she nodded.

Kwan hesitated only a moment. "Let him by." Moving quickly, he approached the lamp and doused the light.

Despite her decision, Saengkeo drew one of the Walthers and eased off the safety. She held the weapon along her leg, slightly behind her thigh.

Stoddard entered the boathouse by the side door Kwan had brought Saengkeo through. The CIA agent glanced around and moved cautiously as the door was closed behind him. Once the door was closed, Kwan switched the lamp back on, flooding Stoddard in light and centering him in the glare. His shadow looked small and narrow on the wall behind him.

"Hey." Stoddard put a hand up in front of his face, trying to block the strong light. "I thought maybe we could talk."

"Secure the perimeter," Kwan ordered over the transceiver. "No one else goes in or out of this area."

The men responded quickly, leaving the slight white noise of the radio silence behind.

Before Saengkeo could respond, Kwan stepped forward and pointed a silenced 9 mm at the center of Stoddard's chest.

"No farther, Agent Stoddard," Kwan said in perfect English.

Stoddard raised his hands and a pained expression twisted

his features. He spoke in perfect Chinese. "Now that's just great, isn't it? You guys stay low-key on the chatter over your radio frequency so nobody knows who you are, then you blab my name around like it was nothing."

"If you weren't certain of absolute deniability or that your agents past the perimeter of my own men couldn't maintain the integrity of this meet," Kwan said, "you wouldn't be here." He paused. "Agent Stoddard."

Stoddard grinned. "You've got me there." He wiggled his hands slowly. "Is it okay if I put my hands down? Or are we going to continue with this charade?"

"I don't know what you're doing here," Saengkeo said, stepping up to match Kwan's position. She made sure she didn't interfere with Kwan's field of fire.

"Why, I came to see you, of course."

"There are other places we could have met."

Stoddard nodded toward the boat. "With the boat hidden here and you coming to see it, I thought maybe this would be the best time. Especially after the way your meeting went this afternoon and early evening."

"How much do you know about the meeting?"

Stoddard shrugged. "Loved the chopstick attack. Huang didn't love it. In fact, he seemed to lack a certain sense of the irony inherent in the situation. But I think you impressed the hell out of Luo. I don't know if you caught the old guy's expression when he first saw Huang stretched out across the table like that, but I can send you a DVD recording."

"No," Saengkeo said. If there were spies for United Bamboo or one of the other triads within her family—and she knew there could well be—having such a recording would be suicidal.

"You should have seen it." Stoddard made a mock surprised expression on his face, then laughed.

Saengkeo watched the man.

"You guys have no sense of humor," Stoddard grumbled. He dropped his hands to his sides and frowned. "To hell with it. My arms are getting tired. If you're going to shoot, shoot."

"No," Saengkeo quickly told Kwan. She wondered if Stoddard knew how close he had come to death in that instant. Then she figured that the CIA agent didn't know or really didn't think Kwan would have killed him.

Kwan said nothing.

Stoddard lowered his head and averted his eyes from the bright light. "Look, you've got to start trusting me and stop playing me for a sap the way you did this morning with Yang. Otherwise we're not going to get anything done. I won't get the chance I need to monitor the triads and the Chinese government as they crawl more and more into bed with each other, and your family won't get out of the criminal activities they're doing."

Saengkeo remained silent.

"Your brother," Stoddard said, "will have died in vain if we don't work together."

"I want to know about this boat," Saengkeo said reluctantly. "I want to know why my brother had this vessel, and how you knew about it being here."

"I can explain the boat," Stoddard promised. "I have to explain the boat."

Arizona

MACK BOLAN DROVE west on Interstate 8, headed for Mexicali. Casa Grande was nearly an hour and a half behind him, and Scottsdale was another hour north of the small town.

The interstate was desolate, a divided highway that had been pounded down in the desert lands of southern Arizona. The moon hung fat and full in the star-filled night sky. Sil-

ver moonlight washed over the barren land, reducing the terrain to a tapestry of light and shadows. The Executioner
caught a momentary flicker of red in a pair of predator's eyes
at the side of the road, and he recognized the tall, lean form
of a coyote as the wind caught tufts of the animal's dark
brown fur.

Bolan listened to a talk radio station, but didn't know what
the host and his guests had been talking about for the past five
or six hours. The conversation had helped keep him awake,
like the off-watch conversations of guys he'd served with.

He nursed an extralarge cup of coffee from the last convenience store he'd filled up at. The insulated mug he'd purchased kept the liquid inside at peak temperature. He'd also
bought a thermos and filled the insulated container from a
fresh pot in the store. During the flight in from New Jersey, he'd
managed to sleep a little, but he knew he was running on empty.

He shifted the cup's lid around to open the spout, then
drank. The coffee remained hot enough to burn his tongue.

The Executioner had left Garcia back in Scottsdale. The
documents forger had proved to be as knowledgeable about
criminal activities in the city as Bolan had believed he would
be. Their first stop had been at a weapon dealer's place of
business. After the brief encounter there, which had left no
one dead, armament wasn't a problem. The man Garcia had
taken the Executioner to supplied military-issue weapons to
survivalists and anarchists. The underground bunker outside
Scottsdale had been a treasure trove of arms. The rental car's
trunk was loaded with gear.

Usually Garcia handled fake documents in batches, all of
the packets prepped and ready for when the snakeheads made
their way into Arizona. This time, though, there had been an
addition at the last minute: a young woman. Bolan had a picture of her in his pocket.

The cell phone connected to the cigarette lighter adapter shrilled for attention.

He picked the handset up and answered, knowing only a handful of people had his current number. "Yeah."

"I have some information on the Chinese end of things," Barbara Price said without preamble.

"Let's hear it."

"What's your twenty? This connection sounds wobbly."

"I'm in between here and there," Bolan replied, listening to the voice transmission fade in and out for a moment, interspersed by the hissing static of white noise. If he hadn't been on the interstate where the cell towers were located regularly, he doubted the phone would have worked at all.

"You haven't made your meet yet?" Price asked, referring to the band of illegal Chinese immigrants reportedly headed in-country.

"No. According to my source, that meet should be only minutes away." Garcia's information included the fact that the Chinese snakeheads were transporting their charges by a two-unit Winnebago team flanked by blockers and support vehicles.

"Any sign of the locals?" Price asked.

The locals were the Immigration and Naturalization Service. "My source says the locals aren't aware of the business."

"I'm not sure that's entirely true," Price said. "I've made a few discreet inquiries tonight about the action in that neck of the woods. I met with some stiff resistance. I think they are aware, and I think that you may encounter them."

Bolan added the probable presence of the INS to the mix. No matter how he added the situation up, the potential was incendiary. "What about the overseas players?"

"I've got nothing more on the shippers yet," Price said, "but we're working to improve that situation now. One of the things that has proved surprising is that the alphabet company you encountered in New York has a heavy buy-in into the local action there."

"What local action?" Bolan asked.

"Family business."

Bolan knew the mission controller was talking about the Chinese triads. He put the information together. According to the facts they'd gathered so far, pirates had taken down the Russian freighter, *Jadviga*. Chinese pirates did business with the triads, but they didn't belong to them.

"The Company team is looking for the lost cargo?" the Executioner asked.

"That's now a primary mission in addition to what the team was already doing there."

"What was the original mission?"

"The Company team was there to establish a liaison within the local families."

Bolan considered that. The Chinese triads were becoming more and more closely aligned with the Communist government. But the soldier had no idea whom the CIA would convince or could coerce into helping the Agency that would be high enough in a triad organization to adequately help. And if someone was high enough in the hierarchy to help, he didn't know what the Agency could offer them. "Who's the liaison?"

"No one knows."

"That's good," Bolan said. If the news had already leaked even to other American intelligence groups—even one as circumspect as Stony Man Farm—whoever the CIA had convinced to help them was only one step away from death. Chances were, that person would be running like a rabbit ahead of a group of blood-crazed hounds.

"Cultivating this liaison has been a long and arduous

process," Price went on. "My access to the project is severely limited."

Bolan guessed that the action was buried so deep that even the various departments within the CIA knew about the attempt to penetrate the triad organizations. "Have they had any success?"

Price hesitated. "All I've got are a few rumors, Striker. And most of those are things I've put together myself rather than anything we've discovered through the ongoing investigation. There have been agents lost over there that may tie to the liaison effort. There has also been some attrition within the crime families' ranks. I can connect the dots from the outside, but there's no conclusive evidence."

"What do you know about the personnel connected to that operation?"

"Almost nothing. I don't want to push too hard on this thing. As you know, with the heat on in Afghanistan and other problems looming in the Middle East, any inquiry directed at that team is going to be the subject of an invasive investigation. I have to maintain the integrity of the operation here, and I've been given orders to stay out of Company business."

"Whose orders?" Bolan asked.

"They came straight from the Man," Price replied.

Bolan considered that. The President didn't warn the Stony Man teams off of much. "Why the special interest?"

"Agency business," Price answered. "You know how he feels about Agency business."

Bolan did know. CIA agents in the Special Activities Division had been the first on the ground in Afghanistan after the events of September 11. One of the President's first acts had been to rename and reclassify the existing Military Support Program as the SAD and use them as the front-line soldiers in his war on terrorism.

"This is a special op, Striker," Price continued. "The kid gloves are off, but the mission is all about finesse."

"The Agency team is looking for the missing cargo?" Bolan asked.

"That's my understanding."

"If the cargo was taken by Chinese pirates like the Russians are saying, maybe the Agency's liaison can turn something up."

"That's what everyone is hoping for," Price agreed. "And if there's a win in the offing, the Man wants the kudos and recognition to go to the Agency. If it does, it'll be good PR. After all, the Man can recognize Agency business."

But Stony Man Farm had to remain invisible. The Executioner understood that.

"Do they know about the woman down here?"

"I don't know."

"Then I'll see if I can make the connect here," Bolan suggested. "Maybe there will be some information we can pass on."

"Understood, Striker."

Either way, Bolan had no intention of bowing out of the mission he'd set for himself. Maybe there were more than three nuclear weapons on the loose in the world at the moment, but he'd targeted the three that had gone missing from *Jadviga*. Until he was ordered to stand down from the operation, he'd ante up and see where the chips fell. Even if he was ordered to stand down, as long as he could make a difference he knew he'd rely on his own judgment.

Bolan watched as a Jeep Cherokee led a pair of older Winnebagos east on Interstate 8. Six motorcycles and two more vehicles, a sedan and a battered Ford pickup, followed the Winnebagos. He scanned the occupants of the vehicles in the quick look afforded as they passed. Soft illumination from dashboard lights illuminated hard features.

The Executioner held his speed steady as he moved his gaze and watched the entourage disappear over the hill in the rearview mirror. "I've got to go," he told Price. "The op here just went green."

"Keep me updated. I'll do what I can from this end."

"Will do," Bolan said, then he broke the connection. He lifted his foot from the accelerator and started to shift to the brake. Before he completed the maneuver, he spotted three full-sized SUVs with whip antennae and Arizona Border Patrol insignias on the door rocketing through the night.

He waited until the Border Patrol vehicles were out of sight, then he switched the rental's lights out and cut across the median, throwing up a cloud of dust. He floored the accelerator and raced in pursuit of the Border Patrol vehicles.

12

Bolan climbed the small rise that had hidden the convoy from him only a moment ago. When he hit the top of the rise, he spotted the three Border Patrol vehicles barreling down on the convoy.

The Border Patrol units didn't try to hide their approach, depending on numbers to intimidate their prey. Almost at the same time, all three vehicles switched on their light bars and the harsh swaths glared through the night.

Reaching under the dashboard, Bolan switched on the police scanner he'd picked up from the arms dealer.

Radio static crackled for a moment, then the channel cleared in a heated rush. "—turned on the lights, but they're not slowing, Blocker One," a man's voice stated.

"Roger that, Tailgate One," another man's voice replied. "Keep 'em coming this way. Maybe those people won't slow there, but we'll take them down here."

The three Border Patrol vehicles closed on the convoy. Immediately, the six motorcycles flared out from the rear Winnebago. The two-wheeled vehicles also slowed, allowing the Border Patrol units to come closer.

Bolan knew the move on the part of the motorcycle teams was a trap.

"Tailgate One," a man said, "I don't like the look of those motorcyclists."

"Don't sweat it," Tailgate One replied confidently. "They're probably just dropping back to make sure that we're who we appear to be. Rival gangs sometimes—"

The rest of the man's words were blasted away by the sudden staccato racket of automatic-weapons fire. Bolan witnessed the long muzzle-flashes jumping from the fists of the passengers on the motorcycles.

"Son of a bitch!" someone swore over the radio frequency. "Blocker! Blocker! They just opened fire on us!"

"Fall back! Fall back!" Blocker replied. "Let 'em come! Let 'em come! We're ready for them here!"

The lead Border Patrol vehicle left the road abruptly, pulling hard to the left as the SUV skidded out of control. For a moment, the vehicle clung tenaciously to the interstate, but when the SUV left the pavement and reached the broken land of the median, it tumbled end over end, bouncing.

"Tailgate One is down!" a man yelled over the radio. "I repeat, Tailgate One is down!"

Grimly, unable to do anything, Bolan watched one of the motorcyclists speed off-road toward the downed SUV as the vehicle rocked to a stop upside down. The passenger flung something toward the SUV. As the motorcycle sped back toward the interstate, the Border Patrol vehicle blew up.

A tall spire of fire and smoke belched into the dark sky.

Two flaming figures crawled weakly from the ruins of the vehicle. Neither of them went far.

Bolan reached into the back seat and lifted the blanket he'd used to cover part of the arsenal he'd gotten from Garcia's contact. He fisted the Mossberg 12-gauge shotgun from the seat and brought the weapon forward as the motorcycle roared up the side of the interstate and went airborne beside him.

The Executioner didn't hesitate. War had been declared by the Chinese snakeheads, and he didn't intend to leave a threat along his backtrail. He cradled the shotgun over his forearm as he shoved the muzzle through the window. He fired on the fly, aiming for the center of the motorcycle and two riders.

The cloud of double-aught buckshot struck the motorcycle driver's crotch and the gas tank at the same time. A fireball wrapped over the two riders in a heated rush as the buckshot knocked the motorcycle sideways. Still, the front wheel slammed against Bolan's rented SUV as the soldier drove past. Hammered by the SUV's greater weight and speed, the motorcycle twisted violently and broke into pieces.

Bolan barely registered the hollow thump of the contact. He gazed at the battlefield before him, hearing the desperation in the Border Patrolmen's voices.

"Blocker, goddammit, they're all over us back here!"

"Hold on!" The man at the other end of the radio frequency sounded anxious. "Back off of them! Don't engage them! I repeat, don't engage them!"

But the engagement had already begun. The motorcyclists smelled blood and went after the Border Patrolmen.

A second Border Patrol unit skidded out of control to the right side of the interstate. Smoke and dust roiled around the vehicle. A moment later, the SUV lurched to a stop. Immediately, two of the motorcyclists went after the SUV like carrion eaters rushing toward a fresh kill. Luckily the Border

Patrolmen in the SUV were well enough to fight back. A blistering hail of gunfire raked one motorcycle clear of riders. The second motorcycle stopped and peeled around in a quick U-turn, speeding back toward the interstate.

Unfortunately the driver never saw Bolan's vehicle rushing out of the darkness. Skillfully the Executioner caught the motorcycle and two gunmen with the front bumper, knocking them aside effortlessly. In the passenger mirror, he caught a glimpse of the motorcycle flipping end over end, spilling the two riders like a bucking bronco. Neither of them got back up.

The last Border Patrol SUV tried desperately to avoid contact with the remaining three motorcycles. Weaving back and forth across the interstate, the driver fought off every attempt the motorcycle riders made to close in on him. The Border Patrol passengers fired at their opponents, succeeding in sending another motorcycle down.

"Blocker, this is Tailgate Two! Where the hell is that chopper?"

"The chopper is en route, Tailgate Two. Just hold tight."

"Tailgate One is toast, Blocker! And Tailgate Three has been taken out of the play! But we've got an unidentified player in a dark SUV coming up fast!"

"Is the bogey friendly?"

"Beats the shit out of me, Blocker! The guy took out two motorcycle teams, so he's good in my book!"

"Maybe he's rival action looking to up our success rate."

"I'll damn well take it tonight!"

Bolan ducked in behind the Border Patrol vehicle, letting the SUV knock the wind off his own for a moment, and got a read on the movement of the remaining motorcyclists. Shifting the shotgun to his left hand, the Executioner tracked a motorcycle sweeping from left to right.

The passenger swept a line of deadly fire across the front of the Border Patrol SUV. Sparks jumped from the top of the vehicle's hood.

When he had the motorcycle passenger in his sights, Bolan dropped the shotgun's muzzle just a little lower and squeezed the trigger. The 12-gauge double-aught blast shredded the motorcycle's rear tire and threw the two-wheeled vehicle out of control immediately. The mangled tire caught in the motorcycle's chain and sprocket, locking the wheel up.

With the wheel locked, the motorcycle skidded for just a moment, then wobbled and fell over. Bolan kept driving straight, running over the broken motorcycle and the two men. Something caught under the SUV's undercarriage, jammed tight between the vehicle and the interstate. A grinding noise filled the SUV's cab as a river of orange sparks spilled in Bolan's wake. Another moment passed and the grinding and the sparks stopped.

The battered Ford pickup fell back on the left while Bolan dodged right to avoid the overlapping fields of fire of the last two motorcycles ahead of him. Without warning, the pickup cut across the traffic lanes and swept into Bolan.

Holding the wheel steady to stay the course, Bolan braced himself for impact. The pickup passenger leaned out of the vehicle and sprayed rounds across the SUV's front. Before the man had more than a dozen shots fired, Bolan lifted the shotgun and blasted the man squarely in the face. The double-aught buckshot ripped the flesh from the man's face and reduced the white bone of the skull to bloody splinters.

Reaching into the back seat again, Bolan found a small canvas bag of grenades, all of them antipersonnel. He pulled the grenade pin, then lobbed the explosive into the Ford's cab. An instant later, as the pickup's driver attempted another metal-crunching attack, the grenade went off.

Bolan caught a momentary glimpse of red-and-white lightning inside the pickup's cab. The force of the explosion blew the windshield out in pieces and ripped the passenger door loose from its hinges. Bubble-shaped dents in the door showed where the antipersonnel payload tried to burst through. The soldier had no doubt that the snakeheads within the pickup were dead. Pilotless, the vehicle careened from the interstate into the median and overturned, driving up a wave of dust and rock.

The two Winnebagos, SUV, sedan and two surviving motorcycles raced over the top of the next rise that was almost invisible in the night-drenched landscape against the black sky. Only the bright peppering of stars demarcated the earth and the heavens.

Topping the ridge, Bolan watched the vehicles try desperately to brake. Lights flared like ruby blisters, but they were embers against the roaring fire of the light bars of half a dozen Border Patrol vehicles on either side of the interstate.

"Blocker!" the radio spit. "This is Tailgate Two! I'm out of the race, but you've still got the bogey coming at you in a dark SUV trailing the targets!"

"Roger that, Tailgate Two. We'll try to keep him out of the way of friendly fire."

"They're not giving up, Blocker! These guys are strictly here for the kill!"

"We'll see how they feel about that when they hit these Stinger Spikes."

Bolan glanced at the interstate ahead of the speeding convoy, barely catching reflected patches of light against the chain of tire-shredding spikes lying there. If he followed the snakehead convoy across the spikes, he knew his own vehicle would be crossing on four flat tires, as well. Escaping across the desert on foot wasn't an alternative.

The Jeep Cherokee leading the convoy was out in front a good six car lengths from the other vehicles. The driver apparently never saw the spikes because he never slowed. As soon as the rubber touched the spikes, the tires went to pieces. Dropping several inches to the interstate, running on rims now and leaving a spray of sparks, the Cherokee continued forward only a short distance, then slewed out of control and overturned.

Downshifting, Bolan shed speed, opting for control. The winking lights of a helicopter came out of the northeast, rocketing toward the roadblock as the Winnebagos, sedan and motorcycle flared out on either side of the roadblock.

"Shit! They're leaving the goddamn road!" a harsh voice called over the radio.

The chains of spikes were designed to end a high-speed chase, but the devices worked only if the targeted perpetrator didn't see them or couldn't think quickly enough to avoid them.

"Aerial, this is Blocker. Do you copy?"

"Aerial copies, Blocker." The helicopter pilot's voice was mixed with the throbbing beat of the rotor wash.

"Maintain a visual."

"Acknowledged, Blocker."

Bolan handled the SUV with care, grateful that the uneven terrain wasn't full of washed-out runnels. The front-end alignment wasn't going to survive the beating, but he remained mobile.

The two Winnebagos went wide of the interstate to the right. Dust clouds trailed them as they sped across the desert floor. One of the Border Patrol units backed out of the pack, obviously intending to block the Winnebagos with the vehicle. Instead, the large recreational vehicle broke the SUV like a child's toy, scattering the twisted remains at the side of the interstate as the driver cut back toward the pavement.

Judging from the way the Winnebago had shaken off the Border Patrol unit, Bolan guessed that the big vehicles had been reinforced. Instead of recreational vehicles, or vessels used for what basically amounted to slave trade, the Winnebagos were something short of tanks.

At the same time, the motorcyclists roared toward the mass of Border Patrol vehicles bunched in the median. Gunfire flared out, yellow tongues strobing the night. Obviously taken by surprise by the death-defying charge of their opponents, the Border Patrol troops reacted slowly. Those who fired their weapons aimed where the snakeheads had already been instead of where they were.

The Chinese triad members chopped into the Border Patrol ranks with their own weapons fire. A moment later, the two motorcycles passed only a few feet from the three vehicles parked in the median. A heartbeat later, an explosion ripped through the cars and the patrolmen taking cover there. Watching the destruction through the cloud of dust left by the fleeing vehicles, Bolan guessed that all of the motorcycle teams were equipped with one or more munitions packets. The snakehead convoy hadn't come up from Mexico with any intention of being easily stopped.

"Aerial, this is Blocker!"

"My God, Blocker, are you guys all right down there?"

The helicopter flew a holding pattern over the attack site, cutting through the roiling clouds of smoke and dust that rose from the desert floor.

"We've got dead and wounded everywhere, Aerial. Call for medevac teams and additional support from base. This run was bigger than what we were led to believe." The man sounded as if he was in shock, teetering on the edge of control. "Stay on that damn convoy! Those bastards aren't going to get away with this!"

Bolan roared around the wreckage of the three Border Patrol vehicles. The air conditioner labored, sucking in smoke and dust despite the filters. For a moment, the Executioner lost sight of the road in the huge dust cloud left by the rolling stock thundering across the desert. When he was on the other side, he spotted the sedan and the two motorcycles pulling onto the interstate behind the two Winnebagos.

"Blocker, we've got two units up and ready to run," a man called over the radio. "We can continue the pursuit."

"Negative. Those units are going to be used as transport vehicles for our wounded. Do not engage those people any further. That's a long stretch of interstate. They can't outrun the radios."

"They can abandon the vehicles, Blocker. And there are small farm-to-market roads they can get lost on."

"Leave the chase up to Aerial. It's in their hands now."

"Roger that. Aerial has pursuit."

High in the air, the helicopter veered away and continued tracking the convoy.

Bolan pulled back onto the interstate and felt the ride immediately smooth. Somewhere along the way cross-country, the windshield had shattered. Bullet holes shone like silvery spiderwebs, but they were dissolving as the safety glass broke free, creating larger and larger holes.

Knowing the windshield had become hazardous, the Executioner locked on the cruise control, then lifted his foot from the accelerator and drove it into the windshield. Two kicks later, the broken glass sheet lifted from the rubber gasket, was caught by the wind, and scraped back over the top of the SUV.

Bolan reached into the console between the seats and took out a pair of aviator sunglasses. When he slid them on, the tint took away some of his night vision but the trade was a good one for the protection the sunglasses provided from the wind.

Lagging behind the sedan by a good fifty yards, the Executioner folded the passenger seat all the way back. He reached into the SUV's rear deck again and took up the Barrett .50-caliber sniper rifle from the collection he'd gotten from the arms dealer. The Barrett had been a surprise, but not too much of one. The heavy-caliber sniping weapon was a favorite among Special Forces soldiers for its range and stopping power.

He'd laid the Barrett in the SUV's rear deck, muzzle forward. Gripping the sniper rifle by the barrel, he dragged the weapon forward. Settling the Barrett over the empty windshield, the Executioner flipped open the scope covers and flicked off the safety.

Keeping both eyes open as he'd been trained to do, Bolan sighted through the scope and kept watch on the interstate at the same time. Luckily the stretch of road was fairly smooth. He laid the crosshairs over the lead motorcyclist, aiming for the center of the mass of men and machine. As long as the bullet touched any part of the intended target, the .50-caliber slug provided the punch to achieve a knockdown.

The Executioner rested his finger on the trigger, let out half a breath and squeezed. The big rifle recoiled into his shoulder but he shrugged off the impact. Seeing that he'd missed the target, knowing that the sound would never reach the men he was aiming at because of the speed they were traveling at and the noise of their machine, he aimed again. He fired, and this time struck one or both of the men.

The motorcycle veered out of control and went down into a flesh-shredding skid at close to one hundred miles per hour. Even if the men lived, Bolan knew they were out of the battle.

The rider on the second motorcycle turned toward Bolan and raised an Uzi. Bright muzzle-flashes leaped from the weapon's barrel, but the sound was lost against the whistle of the wind invading the SUV and the straining engine.

Aiming on the fly, trusting his instincts, Bolan squeezed the trigger. The bullet caught the outer edge of the target, hammering into the back of the motorcycle driver's helmet. Out of control with a dead man doing the steering, the motorcycle went down, veering into the path of the approaching sedan.

The sedan's brakes flared as the driver tried to avoid the collision. Before the sedan could get clear, the motorcycle slid up underneath. Caught on high center, the sedan slid toward the right embankment and went off-road. For a moment the driver didn't look as if he would get the sedan back under control. Then the motorcycle wreckage and corpses cleared and he steered back for the interstate.

Leaving the Barrett butt-down in the passenger seat with the muzzle thrusting through the empty windshield space, Bolan took up one of the two Desert Eagles he'd gotten from the arms dealer. The big Israeli Arms .44 Magnum pistol came up like a natural extension of the Executioner's arm as he drew even with the sedan struggling to pull back onto the interstate.

Bolan held his fire until he clearly saw the driver's face through the side window, then he pulled the trigger. The Desert Eagle bucked in his fist, and he rode out the recoil. The .44 boat-tail slugs rocketed through the SUV's closed window, blowing glass away, then punching through the sedan's window.

Deformed from the collisions with the two panes of glass, the .44 rounds ripped the driver's head from his shoulders. A shadow in the passenger seat made a frantic grab for the wheel, but the sedan left the road again and overturned.

"Aerial," the radio blared, "do you still have visual contact?"

"Affirmative, Blocker. Your bogey is chewing through the Chinese traffickers like there was no tomorrow. The only vehicles left up and running are the two Winnebagos."

"Have you made an ID on him?"

"Negative. I'm staying locked on to the Winnebagos. Maybe we'll have a meet after this is over. Whoever the guy is, he's a pro."

Bolan reloaded the Desert Eagle and stuffed the pistol between his seat and the console. He took up the Barrett. The sniper rifle contained eleven rounds in a full magazine, and nine were still locked and loaded. Movement atop the rear Winnebago drew his attention.

A man climbed up through a roof access panel and lay flat on top of the Winnebago. Slipping a long tube from over his shoulder, the man rolled to his side and took aim.

Recognizing the RPG-7 rocket launcher, Bolan scooped up the cell phone and punched the number for the Arizona State Police.

"Arizona State Police," a woman's voice answered.

"There's a Border Patrol engagement ongoing with a group of Chinese illegal-immigrant traffickers," Bolan said.

"Sir, your call isn't registering on my trace."

"Warn the helicopter pilot that the traffickers have a rocket launcher," Bolan went on, ignoring the protest. His cell phone wasn't registering because the device was a clone. "Back him off. Now."

"Sir, I need you to identify yourself. Give me your location."

Bolan broke the connection. He'd done all he could do.

"Blocker, this is Aerial. Looks like one of the Winnebago teams has a man on the roof. I'm going in for a closer look.

Maybe we can get one of these bastards on video and ID him later if they escape."

Reaching for the Barrett, Bolan snugged the sniper rifle to his shoulder again. He sighted through the scope and fired, missing the man lying atop the recreational vehicle.

The helicopter swooped down like a descending hawk, shedding altitude and closing on the Winnebago. Less than one hundred feet out, even as Bolan was squeezing off a third shot that struck sparks from the top rear of the Winnebago, the man with the RPG-7 fired.

The rocket leaped from the launcher and knifed through the night. For a moment, Bolan thought the rocket had missed the helicopter, then an explosion flared up from the landing gear. The explosion swept on up into the helicopter, expanding as the gas tanks ruptured and caught fire.

In a heartbeat, the helicopter took on the aspects of a Roman candle, mushrooming into a ball of twisting flames and ember-filled smoke. Then the aircraft fell, coming back toward Bolan.

Taking the steering wheel in both hands, the Executioner pulled hard to the left, narrowly avoiding the plummeting mass of the destroyed helicopter. Burning embers threaded through the empty windshield space and floated through the SUV like angry fireflies before winking out. The soldier felt the heat of the flaming craft against the right side of his face. Flames licked at the passenger door, curling against the window.

Then he was past the wreckage fouling the interstate, still locked in pursuit of the two Winnebagos.

The man atop the rear Winnebago lifted the rocket launcher again and took aim.

Bolan saw reflections of the burning helicopter in his side mirrors as he lifted the Barrett. He steadied the SUV, knowing he was making an easier target for the man with the rocket launcher even as he improved his own chances.

The rocket launcher ignited, spewing flames, as Bolan locked on to the man's face. The deadly payload slammed into the interstate only a few feet ahead and to the soldier's left. Heat coiled within the concussive wave that broke across the SUV. His tires came within inches of the crater that opened up in the road.

Holding his target, both eyes open, the Executioner stroked the trigger. The .50-caliber bullet sliced across the distance and struck the man in the face. All motor control left the corpse at once. Loose-limbed and propelled by the rush of wind, the dead man tumbled across the Winnebago rooftop and fell.

"Aerial! Aerial, this is Blocker! Do you copy?"

Bolan shoved the Barrett aside. The burning helicopter was a small image in his mirrors now.

"Aerial!"

Turning his full attention to the takedown of the two Winnebagos, knowing the vehicles held innocents aboard, as well as enemies, the Executioner took up the Mossberg and put his foot down harder on the accelerator. Most of the damage the SUV had suffered was superficial. The vehicle surged in response.

From thirty feet out, Bolan fired the shotgun three times, putting all the spreads into the engine area. The Winnebagos were pusher vehicles, designed with the diesel engines mounted in the rear instead of in the front. There was a slim chance that the buckshot would penetrate the engine compartment, and the risk was something he had to take. If he didn't stop the Winnebagos, the people aboard were destined for virtual slavery somewhere. Deportation back to their home country was preferable to death.

The sheet metal collapsed under the onslaught of buckshot. The engine started smoking and the Winnebago slowed instantly, encouraging Bolan to believe that he'd shut down the power plant.

Glancing forward, the soldier saw brakelights flare on the other Winnebago. As the stricken recreational vehicle slowed even more, the other Winnebago came around in a turn.

Knowing he had no choice except to seize the moment, Bolan passed the first Winnebago and brought the SUV around in a tight turn. Dust and smoke coasted in from the rear of the Winnebago, obscuring him for a moment. His eyes and throat burned from the toxic fumes.

He took the Desert Eagle from beside the seat and shoved the weapon into the holster on the combat harness he'd readied for the confrontation. Already in motion, dressed in black, the Executioner seized the M-16/M-203 combo and a Kevlar vest from the back seat. He trotted to the SUV's rear, pulling the combat harness on over the Kevlar vest.

A Chinese gunner stepped from the recreational vehicle cradling an Uzi machine pistol. A line of 9 mm rounds sprayed the front of the SUV to Bolan's right.

Moving on instinct trained by years of war and sudden death, the Executioner lifted the M-16 and hammered two 3-round bursts into the man's chest. The trafficker stutter-stepped back and sprawled across the interstate.

A shadow moved behind the driver's side of the Winnebago's windshield.

Identifying the driver as the man leveled a machine pistol, Bolan put a 3-round burst into the trafficker's chest. The tumbling 5.56 mm rounds wouldn't penetrate the man or the driver's compartment and would leave the human cargo safe from harm.

On the move now, the Executioner pulled a CS canister free of the combat webbing. After arming the device, Bolan heaved the grenade through the shattered glass of the windshield. He caught another trafficker stepping down out of the Winnebago, moving so quickly that the man didn't even know he was there. Bolan buttstroked the man with the assault rifle.

Bone shattered and the man sagged in the doorway just as the CS canister went off with a dulled pop.

Bolan reached up and caught the unconscious trafficker's shirtfront, hauling the man from the RV and heaving him out onto the interstate. The soldier grabbed the gas mask he'd mounted on the combat harness in readiness and pulled the straps over his head.

White CS gas billowed out of the canister on the Winnebago's floor, the hissing mixing with the shrill screams and panicked cries of the men and women inside the vehicle. A moment later, the screams and cries died away for the most part, replaced by the choking effects of the gas.

Clad in the mask, Bolan vaulted up the short flight of steps into the RV. He doubted there were many armed men aboard the vehicle. Space on the Winnebago was limited and translated into dollars. Three men were already down.

Lights cut through the shattered windshield as Bolan turned and stared into the Winnebago's interior. The other RV had arrived, and the soldier knew the traffickers were already disembarking. The rescue time was measured in heartbeats.

The tear gas spun and shifted in layers inside the RV. More than twenty people occupied the hollowed-out vehicle's interior. All of them lay on the floor, scared and overcome by the debilitating gas.

One man, though, held a young woman in front of him, his forearm wrapped tightly across her throat. He held a pistol to her temple. The man sat on the floor, making himself a small target behind his shield.

Nuclear Game

"Go away," the man warned in broken English. He hacked and coughed. "Go away or I kill this bitch."

As smooth as mercury at room temperature, Bolan fired two rounds into the man's exposed shoulder. The pistol dropped from the trafficker's useless arm, and he opened his mouth to scream in pain. The Executioner fired again, stitching a 3-round burst that started in the man's open mouth and tracked up to the top of his head.

The young woman the trafficker had been holding screamed in wide-eyed terror. She gazed down at the dead man's blood covering her.

Only immigrants remained in the Winnebago.

Bolan raked his gaze over the people huddled on the vehicle's floor, searching for the face he had committed to memory. No one looked like they normally did with the effects the tear gas had on them.

Voices called out from the interstate outside.

13

Shifting his attention back to the threat of the Chinese snake-head approaching outside the Winnebago, Bolan returned to the front of the RV. He stayed out of view, pulled a high-explosive grenade from his combat harness, slipped the spoon and counted down, then threw the grenade toward three armed traffickers.

The grenade bounced once in front of the traffickers and was a foot off the ground when the explosion took place. Thunder roared across the interstate as the men flew backward. When the traffickers hit the ground, they didn't move again.

A fusillade of bullets struck the RV's interior. By then, the Executioner was already on the move. He knew the M-16 held only half a clip. Three men were down. He'd counted seven, and he didn't think there were any more.

Outside the RV, the soldier dashed forward and halted at the front bumper. He swung around, staying low and dropping the M-16 into target acquisition. Squeezing the trigger, he emptied the last of the assault rifle's rounds into a pair of traffickers who had almost reached the RV. The 5.56 mm tumblers caught the men in midstride and hammered them backward.

The remaining two men froze like deer in headlights for a moment, knowing they'd run out of luck.

Bolan reached for the M-203's trigger as the men tried to bring their weapons to bear. When he squeezed the trigger, the grenade launcher belched a 40 mm HE warhead that struck the man on the left in the chest.

The blast husked the trafficker, emptying his chest cavity in a heated rush that tore his torso from his waist in the next instant.

Releasing the assault rifle with his right hand, Bolan drew the Desert Eagle from the holster at the side of the combat harness. The trafficker got off two shots that struck the front of the RV at Bolan's side and cut the air beside his head. Moving naturally into a Weaver's stance as a defensive precaution, the Executioner lifted the Desert Eagle and started firing. The first .44 Magnum round caught the man in the crotch, and the following bullets worked steadily up to their target's chin.

With the last of his enemies down, Bolan reloaded his weapons as he trotted toward the second Winnebago and climbed in, senses alert.

The illegal immigrants cowered in the big RV, clinging to the floor and not looking at the big man. The woman he was looking for was half the length of the Winnebago back. Besides her features, the other thing that made her stand out from the other people in the RV was the handcuffs chaining her to the wall.

She was the only true prisoner aboard the RV.

Bolan stepped toward the woman. "What's your name?" he growled.

The woman shook her head and tried to hide her face in the crook of her arm.

"I need to talk to you," Bolan said.

"Leave me alone," the woman replied. Fear cracked in her voice.

"I can't," Bolan said. He lifted the Desert Eagle, watching her cringe and try to escape him. He fired and the Magnum round split the chain holding the handcuffs before exiting the vehicle through the wall. Shouldering the M-16, he grabbed her by the arm and hustled her toward the door.

She fought against him, crying out for help, but none of the other people tried to intervene.

"Calm down," Bolan said. "I'm not going to hurt you."

Outside the RV, she tried to run. When Bolan got hold of her again, she fought, launching martial-arts kicks and swinging her manacled fists. Slipping behind her, the soldier looped his free arm under her chin and locked her in a sleeper hold. Only seconds later, she passed out from lack of oxygen to her brain. He caught her limp body and draped her over his shoulder, then carried her to the waiting SUV.

After securing the woman in the passenger seat and using duct tape to bind her hands behind the seat, Bolan slid behind the steering wheel. He surveyed the battle zone, knowing the Border Patrol and the Arizona State Police would be arriving soon. He had to be long gone by then.

As he got under way, Bolan glanced at the unconscious woman beside him, wondering what secrets she held and how they might tie in with three Russian nuclear weapons that had gone missing somewhere off the China coast.

* * * * *

Don't miss Executioner #297,
DEADLY PURSUIT, Volume II in the exciting
MOON SHADOW *trilogy.*

THE Destroyer®

TROUBLED WATERS

Thomas "Captain" Kidd is the new scourge of the Caribbean, and when he and his crew kidnap the daughter of a senator, CURE sets out to kick some serious pirate booty. Posing as rich tourists, Remo and Chiun set a course for the tropics to tempt these freebooters into the mistake of their career. But Remo soon finds himself swimming with sharks, while Chiun senses some illicit treasure in his future. Even so, they are ready to dispatch the sea raiders to an afterlife between the devil and the deep blue sea.

Available in October 2003 at your favorite retail outlet.

Or order your copy now by sending your name, address, zip or postal code, along with a check or money order (please do not send cash) for $6.50 for each book ordered ($7.99 in Canada), plus 75¢ postage and handling ($1.00 in Canada), payable to Gold Eagle Books, to:

In the U.S.	In Canada
Gold Eagle Books	Gold Eagle Books
3010 Walden Avenue	P.O. Box 636
P.O. Box 9077	Fort Erie, Ontario
Buffalo, NY 14269-9077	L2A 5X3

Please specify book title with your order.
Canadian residents add applicable federal and provincial taxes.

GOLD EAGLE®

GDEST133

Take
2 explosive books
plus a
mystery bonus
FREE

Mail to: Gold Eagle Reader Service™

IN U.S.A.:
3010 Walden Ave.
P.O. Box 1867
Buffalo, NY 14240-1867

IN CANADA:
P.O. Box 609
Fort Erie, Ontario
L2A 5X3

YEAH! Rush me 2 FREE Gold Eagle® novels and my FREE mystery bonus. If I don't cancel, I will receive 6 hot-off-the-press novels every other month. Bill me at the low price of just $29.94* for each shipment. That's a savings of over 10% off the combined cover prices, and there is NO extra charge for shipping and handling! There is no minimum number of books I must buy. I can always cancel at any time simply by returning a shipment at your cost or by returning any shipping statement marked "cancel." Even if I never buy another book from Gold Eagle, the 2 free books and mystery bonus are mine to keep forever.

166 ADN DNU4
366 ADN DNU5

Name _____ (PLEASE PRINT) _____

Address _____ Apt. No. _____

City _____ State/Prov. _____ Zip/Postal Code _____

Signature (if under 18, parent or guardian must sign)

* Terms and prices subject to change without notice. Sales tax applicable in N.Y. Canadian residents will be charged applicable provincial taxes and GST. This offer is limited to one order per household and not valid to present Gold Eagle® subscribers. All orders subject to approval.

® are registered trademarks of Harlequin Enterprises Limited
GE2-02

Stony Man is deployed against an armed
invasion on American soil...

AXIS OF CONFLICT

The free world's worst enemy failed to destroy her once
before, but now they've regrouped and expanded—a jihad
vengeance that is nothing short of bio-engineered
Armageddon, brilliant and unstoppable. A weapon unlike
anything America has ever seen is about to be unleashed on
U.S. soil. Stony Man races across the globe in a desperate
bid to halt a vision straight out of doomsday—with
humanity's extinction on the horizon....

STONY MAN

*Available in
August 2003
at your favorite
retail outlet.*

Or order your copy now by sending your name, address, zip or postal code, along with
a check or money order (please do not send cash) for $6.50 for each book ordered
($7.99 in Canada), plus 75¢ postage and handling ($1.00 in Canada), payable to Gold
Eagle Books, to:

In the U.S.	In Canada
Gold Eagle Books	Gold Eagle Books
3010 Walden Avenue	P.O. Box 636
P.O. Box 9077	Fort Erie, Ontario
Buffalo, NY 14269-9077	L2A 5X3

Please specify book title with your order.
Canadian residents add applicable federal and provincial taxes.

GOLD
EAGLE®

GSM66

Readers won't want to miss this exciting new title of the SuperBolan series!

Don Pendleton's Mack Bolan

Breached

Barely surviving the opening salvo in a brutal new war to seize control of the drug supply through America's border pipeline, Mack Bolan resumes his offensive to neutralize the operations of a powerful Chinese Triad and a Mexican drug cartel. Both factions are going down, the hard way, and Bolan's front lines span Nevada, Toronto and Hong Kong.

Available in September 2003 at your favorite retail outlet.

Or order your copy now by sending your name, address, zip or postal code, along with a check or money order (please do not send cash) for $6.50 for each book ordered ($7.99 in Canada), plus 75¢ postage and handling ($1.00 in Canada), payable to Gold Eagle Books, to:

In the U.S.	**In Canada**
Gold Eagle Books	Gold Eagle Books
3010 Walden Avenue	P.O. Box 636
P.O. Box 9077	Fort Erie, Ontario
Buffalo, NY 14269-9077	L2A 5X3

Please specify book title with your order.
Canadian residents add applicable federal and provincial taxes.

GOLD EAGLE

GSB92